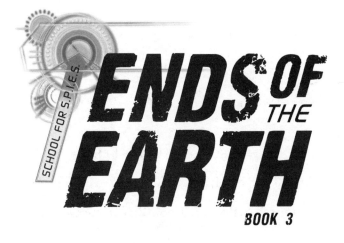

SCHOOL FOR S.P.I.E.S.

ENDS OF THE EARTH

BOOK 3

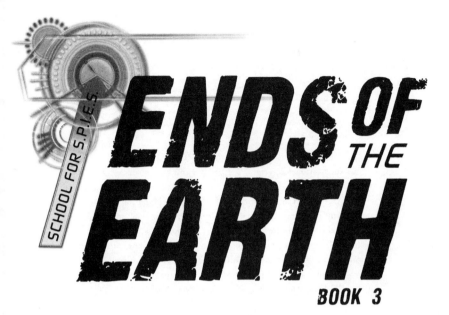

SCHOOL FOR S.P.I.E.S.

ENDS OF THE EARTH

BOOK 3

BRUCE HALE

WITH ILLUSTRATIONS BY

BRANDON DORMAN

Disney • Hyperion

Los Angeles   New York

First Edition, June 2015
1 3 5 7 9 10 8 6 4 2
G475-5664-5-15105

Printed in the United States of America

Library of Congress Cataloging-in-Publication Data
Hale, Bruce.
Ends of the earth/by Bruce Hale.—First edition.
pages cm.—(School for S.P.I.E.S.; book 3)
Summary: To stop LOTUS from taking over the government with its mind-control
device, reluctant spy Max Segredo must reunite with his father and orphan friends.
ISBN 978-1-4231-6852-2
[1. Spies—Fiction. 2. Brainwashing—Fiction. 3. Orphans—Fiction.
4. Racially mixed people—Fiction.] I. Title.
PZ7.H1295En 2015
[Fic]—dc23   2014033471

Reinforced binding

Visit www.DisneyBooks.com

SUSTAINABLE FORESTRY INITIATIVE   Certified Sourcing
www.sfiprogram.org
SFI-00993

THIS LABEL APPLIES TO TEXT STOCK

This one's for Carole and Terry

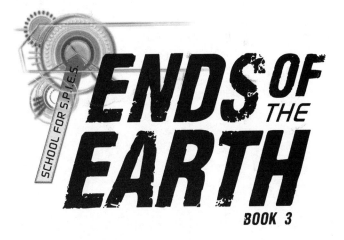

SCHOOL FOR S.P.I.E.S.

ENDS OF THE EARTH

BOOK 3

HOW TO SNATCH A BOY GENIUS

MAX SEGREDO was quietly going stark, raving bonkers. Not only was his orphanage home destroyed and everyone he cared about missing, maybe even dead, but now he was working with the very people responsible for wrecking his life.

Stressful? Oh, just a tad. Frustrating? You might say that.

Having to smile and nod and pretend to support LOTUS's wicked plans after what they'd done to him was enough to make *anyone* go bonkers. Being a double agent, Max reflected, was definitely not for the faint of heart.

Max was sitting with two LOTUS spies in an unmarked van, on a quiet side street, waiting to kidnap a boy genius named Addison Rook. It was the sort of classic spy mission most agents would leap at. Not Max. All he wanted now was to be a normal kid with a normal family—far, far away from there.

3

But duty was duty, especially when the person who had sent you undercover was the closest thing you had to a mother.

"I can't believe the guv'nor trusted you with this job," muttered Humphrey Wall from the driver's seat. A mahogany-brown, V-shaped man, he wore a perpetually pinched expression that made him look like an evil catalog model with intestinal distress.

"Why *not* trust me?" said Max. "I've got an honest face."

"And a devious little mind," said Dijon LeStrange, the van's third occupant. With her honey-blond hair and pale skin, she was the perfect complement to Humphrey—lovely and lethal, as hard as a fistful of brass knuckles.

"Hey, I joined LOTUS of my own free will," said Max.

"Sure," Dijon drawled. "After we chased you halfway across the city and cornered you on a rooftop."

Max shrugged, his face carefully blank. "My mistake. I thought you were child welfare workers."

The walkie-talkie in Dijon's hand crackled with static. A deep voice rumbled, "C Team, status update?"

"Ready to roll," said Dijon.

"And the boy?" said the radio voice, which Max knew belonged to an über-spy named Ebelskeever.

Dijon glanced back over her shoulder at Max and sneered. "Ready as he'll ever be. Looks exactly like a private-school prat."

"Hey," Max objected. But without much heat. He sported the uniform—blue blazer, hideous maroon tie, and gray trousers—that the boys at Addison Rook's school wore. And in this getup, he had to admit, he did feel rather pratlike.

Max stifled a sigh. The mood in the LOTUS van was as tense and serious as a daylong dental surgery, so unlike the buoyant team spirit that had marked his previous missions for S.P.I.E.S. But those days were behind him now. Perhaps forever.

His mind drifted as Ebelskeever checked in with the other units. Even several days after LOTUS's devastating raid on his group's safe house, Max still couldn't believe that S.P.I.E.S. (Systematic Protection, Intelligence, & Espionage Services—and yes, a rather obvious name for a spy organization) was no more.

He could almost hear his spymaster—brusque, bighearted Hantai Annie Wong—chiding him for his sentimentality. She was the one, after all, who had ordered him to join LOTUS if the opportunity arose, and bring them down from the inside. But she'd never told him what to do if S.P.I.E.S. itself dissolved. That last twist was making it very difficult for Max to focus on his mission.

Instead, he kept recalling Cinnabar's golden eyes, Wyatt's cheerful attitude, Mr. Stones's teasing sarcasm. Would he never experience these things, never see his friends, again? How was it possible to find and lose a family so quickly?

Humphrey's gruff voice interrupted his reverie. "Look lively, boy. The pigeon's on the move."

Max peered through the windshield at the intersection just ahead. Any minute now, Addison Rook would motor past in his sporty red BMW. Any minute now, the four LOTUS teams would spring into action like a ravenous wolf pack descending on a baby bunny.

The boy genius didn't stand a chance.

Scooting over on the bench seat, Max rested a hand on the door latch. He felt a pang as strong as hunger, a longing to slip outside and disappear into the gloomy November morning—far from Humphrey, Dijon, and the rest of their corrupt organization. Even an uncaring foster family would be an improvement. All he had to do was step out the door and . . .

"Here he comes," growled Ebelskeever on the radio. "C Team, release Segredo."

"Copy that," said Dijon.

Humphrey half turned in the seat to glare at him. "You're up, boy. And don't try nuffin' funny."

"What, like my Bart Simpson impression?" said Max.

The broad-shouldered man glowered. "You know what I mean. If we have to come chase you, I'll be right peeved."

Max snapped off a mock salute and opened the door.

"Be a good little spy," Dijon drawled, as if she could read his mind. "We'll be watching."

The brisk morning air smelled of wood smoke and decaying leaves as Max scuffed his way up the sidewalk, book bag slung over one shoulder. It rankled that they didn't trust him. True, he *did* intend to destroy their organization, but *they* didn't know that.

Again, the urge to flee fluttered in his chest like a caged hummingbird. Despite their threats, he could probably lose the LOTUS agents in this rambling neighborhood of grand houses and stately trees. But for all Max knew, they'd slipped a tracking device into his clothes, and besides, if he ran now, he wouldn't be able to use LOTUS's considerable resources to locate his friends. In his mind's eye, he pictured Hantai Annie saying one of her favorite phrases: *"Gambare*—go for it.*"* Wherever she was—assuming she was still alive—she was counting on him to fulfill his mission and find her again. So, somehow, he resisted his impulse to run.

Max shook his head. Too bad there wasn't a textbook on the subject of operating undercover all by oneself. A little help from *The Dummy's Guide to Double Agents* would come in quite handy about now.

He approached the intersection. This route lay only five blocks away from Addison Rook's posh private school, but it was out of the main flow of morning commuters. LOTUS had picked their ambush spot with care.

And sure enough, only a sleepy dad in a shiny Peugeot could be seen on the road. Max reached the corner and glanced right. Here they came: LOTUS's lead car, a charcoal-gray Mercedes, followed by Addison's BMW. They tooled past him, and brake lights flared as the vehicles slowed for the stop sign a half block down.

Almost against his will, Max's pulse quickened and his senses sharpened. True, he was only pretending to work for the bad guys, but a mission was a mission, after all.

He strolled up the sidewalk toward the cars. The Mercedes had stopped dead at the intersection. After a couple of seconds, the Beamer's horn blasted, but the other vehicle didn't budge.

Before Addison's car could reverse and pull around it, a second LOTUS Mercedes, this one quartz blue, zipped past Max and squealed to a stop, barely tapping the BMW's rear bumper. Now Addison was trapped, a regular whiz-kid sandwich.

Doors flew open on the LOTUS cars, and four agents in dusk-colored suits sprang out. Despite himself, Max admired the efficiency of the operation. Everything was unfolding with Swiss-watch timing, just as LOTUS's chief, Mrs. Frost, had planned.

Then the watch popped its first spring.

Gunfire crackled from a rear window of the Beamer, and the LOTUS agents dodged back, surprised. Max squinted at the BMW. LOTUS surveillance had gotten it wrong. Addison wasn't alone.

Now the curbside door burst open and a beefy Asian man with a buzz cut leaped out, weapon raised. Max recognized Lizard Eyes, his private nickname for Addison's puffy-eyed bodyguard. He'd seen the man only last week, during S.P.I.E.S.'s mission to steal a mind-control device from Addison's parents. The mission had been successful—if you didn't count the fact that LOTUS had hijacked the invention for itself.

"Back off," cried the bodyguard, covering the agents with his pistol. "And maybe I won't kill you."

A pale, spiky-haired teen dressed like Max climbed out of the other rear door.

Lizard Eyes's head swiveled toward him. "Addison! Back in the car!"

Seizing on the distraction, one of the LOTUS agents whipped his arm forward. The bodyguard grunted and dropped his gun. A ninja throwing star, or *shuriken*, was now protruding from his forearm. The four spies rushed forward to grapple with Lizard Eyes and the white chauffeur.

Eyes wide, Addison backpedaled away from the melee. It appeared as though the spies hadn't noticed him yet.

"Oi!" Max called, stepping into the street. "Over here!"

The teen glanced his way, and Max beckoned.

"I, er . . ." Addison frowned, hesitating. He looked as befuddled as a mongoose on ice.

Really? The kid couldn't choose between being captured

by bad guys and fleeing with a fellow student? Some genius.

"Run!" cried Max. He hustled across the street, toward a narrow alleyway between two houses, and gestured again.

At last, Addison recognized his predicament. He lurched into action, galumphing across the street to join Max. "What—?" he called.

"This way!" said Max, pulling at the other boy's sleeve. "We've got to ditch them."

Then LOTUS's Swiss-watch plan blew a ratchet wheel.

With the wail of a siren, a blue-and-yellow-checked police car rounded the corner and squealed to a stop, blocking the first Mercedes. Two constables jumped out and leveled their Tasers over the top of their doors.

"Freeze!" cried the larger cop.

Addison wheeled around and took a halting step toward the police car. Max grimaced. The plan was falling apart!

Relief and worry warred in Max's mind. Worry won. He caught Addison's arm and spun him back. "No!"

"Why not?" said the boy genius. "They're—"

"They could be in on it," Max improvised.

Addison's lip curled. "You're dead from the neck up," he scoffed.

"What, um, better way to separate you from your bodyguard? Everyone trusts cops." Only with great effort did Max keep from wincing at his own words. It was one of the flimsiest explanations he'd ever concocted, and he'd concocted quite a few.

The teen wavered. The boom of gunshots decided him.

"Right, then. Follow me!" said Addison, trying to make it seem as though he was in charge.

Max rolled his eyes and trailed the older boy down the alley.

The brick walls rose beside them, and the pair splashed through puddles left by last night's rain. In short order, Max could tell the boy genius was more accustomed to exercising his mind than his body. The teen's pace grew as ragged as a pair of hand-me-down jeans. Just halfway along the passage, Addison slowed and glanced back at Max.

"Do I . . . know you?" he panted.

"Seen you around," said Max. He glanced behind them. "Let's keep moving."

After a few more staggering paces, the teen slowed and turned back again. "Why are you . . . helping me?" he asked.

Max suppressed a surge of irritation and kept his expression open and concerned. "We go to the same school, don't we? Can't let some blokes kidnap a fellow Badger."

Addison frowned. "But our mascot's the hedgehog."

"Right," said Max. "I always get those two confused. Now come on." He hooked Addison's elbow and hurried him along.

But the older boy wasn't finished with question time. His steps dragged even more. "Where are you taking me?"

"Someplace safe," said Max, "where we can hide out and call the real cops."

"But why—?"

"Let's *go!*" Max snapped. "They could be right behind us."

This thought spurred Addison back into action. Chalk-faced, he kept shooting glances behind them, as Max half dragged him down the alley.

"I don't get . . . much exercise," panted the boy genius.

"Really?" Max managed with a straight face. "Wouldn't have guessed."

At last, the end of the narrow passage appeared, but instead of a cross street, the boys glimpsed a ramp leading up to a shadowy doorway.

"Oh, no." Addison faltered. "A dead end?"

"A safe hideout," said Max, tugging the older boy up the ramp. The door was unlocked and swung open to his touch. The interior was dim.

Right on the threshold, Addison balked, a belated warning firing from his reptilian brain.

"Now see here," he blustered. "I—"

Max had had enough. Planting his palms on Addison's back, he shoved hard. "In you go!"

A massive, shadowy form seized the boy genius. A hypodermic syringe glinted in a stray beam of light.

"And down you go," rumbled Mr. Ebelskeever.

A TOUCH OF FROST

MAX DARTED through the doorway and caught Addison under the arms as he slumped like a string-snipped marionette, unconscious. Ebelskeever stepped around them and closed the false-front door. A second LOTUS agent snapped on a work light, and in its harsh illumination Max saw that they stood in the cargo compartment of a good-size truck with its back end up against the partition.

Before he'd known Ebelskeever's name, Max had privately dubbed him Gorilla Man; now that he knew the agent better, he realized that name was unfair. Gorillas were gentle giants. Ebelskeever, however, was a mass of murderous muscle—all brawny shoulders and killer instincts.

The big man hammered on the front wall of the cargo space. "Give us some room!" he boomed. The engine turned over and the truck rolled forward several feet, leaving a gap between the rear bumper and the fake wall.

"Seems like an awful lot of trouble just to kidnap one lousy boy genius," said Max. He braced himself against Addison's weight. The teen was heavier than he looked.

Ebelskeever barked a laugh. "And how else do you reckon we convince his parents to make us a new headpiece for the brain-control thingie? Ask 'em pretty please?"

"Well, I—"

"After you so carelessly took the bloody thing for a dip in the river?" Ebelskeever's black eyes flashed under his heavy brow and his lips pressed flat. Did he know Max was a double agent?

The other agent, a bronze-skinned woman with pale green eyes, slipped her arms under Addison's armpits and relieved Max of his burden.

"Get his feet," she snapped.

"I didn't mean to wreck it," Max muttered to Ebelskeever as he and Green Eyes carried the unconscious teen over to a gurney and strapped him down. In a way, that was true—Max hadn't intentionally destroyed that critical part of the invention; he had merely wanted to keep it away from LOTUS.

And now LOTUS had sorted out a way to obtain a replacement headset and make their brain-control device operational. Just a little friendly kidnapping, some gunplay on a suburban street, and then—hey, presto!—a new headpiece.

Next stop: world domination.

The massive man pounded twice on the truck cab's inner wall. "Switch!" he bellowed. Max heard the truck's cab door open. "Come on, Segredo. You're riding up front with me, where I can keep an eye on you."

Max and Ebelskeever hopped out of the rear of the cargo compartment. After a third LOTUS agent stepped around the side of the truck and joined Green Eyes in the back, he and the big man pulled the truck's rear panel down and secured it.

"We're leaving this fake wall and door?" asked Max, jerking his head at the barrier behind them.

"Yup."

"Won't someone be suspicious?"

"Not our problem," said Ebelskeever. "Let's go."

When Max opened the truck's passenger-side door, he froze in his tracks.

"Hi, Max."

A lithe blond girl with toffee-brown eyes sat in the middle of the bench seat, her hands in her lap.

"Vespa," Max croaked. His throat tightened and conflicting emotions ricocheted around his belly like a Ping-Pong ball in an Olympic finals match. Until he met Vespa da Costa, Max hadn't known it was possible to like and loathe someone at the same time. "What are *you* doing here?" he choked out. Even gazing at her lovely face pained him, because each time he saw it, her betrayal sprang to mind.

"My aunt." Vespa glanced over at him with a mixture of guilt and something else he couldn't read. "She wanted me to observe."

Her aunt being Mrs. Frost, the ruthless old woman who ran LOTUS's British division. The one to whom Vespa had spilled all of S.P.I.E.S.'s secrets.

"Oh," said Max.

Ebelskeever slammed the driver-side door and growled, "Hop in, Romeo. Unless you fancy explaining yourself to the coppers."

Shoulders tensed, Max slowly climbed into the cab. Before he'd even fastened his safety belt, the vehicle ground into gear, bumping out of the alley and onto a street. Shifted by momentum, Vespa's warm weight pressed against his side for a second. The scent of tropical flowers teased his nose, and her eyes flicked over to him and then away as she righted herself.

Max set his jaw, deciding to say nothing. He'd mostly been able to avoid her during his few days at LOTUS's headquarters in the capital. No reason that practice shouldn't continue.

But Vespa had other ideas.

"Max, we need to talk," she said.

"Actually," he said, "we don't."

She shifted on the seat to face him. "You can't just keep avoiding me."

"Watch me."

Vespa's eyes were huge and shiny. "Please?"

A hot spike of anger flared in Max's gut. "Really? You want to do this right here and now?" His gaze took in Ebelskeever's bulk on Vespa's other side.

The burly spy chuckled. "Don't mind me, lovebirds. I couldn't care less about your little spat."

He stopped the truck at an intersection. Looking past him, Max could see the spot where the snatch had taken place. Now two police constables had a LOTUS agent cuffed and leaning up against the gray Mercedes. There was no sign of the other LOTUS car, or of the other agents.

"Pity about old Desmond," said Ebelskeever with a wry headshake. "He always was a bit slow off the mark."

The truck wheeled away and jounced down the road with its kidnapped cargo in the back. Ebelskeever's musky odor (like a wolverine in heat mixed with a men's locker room) filled the cab, smothering Vespa's distracting floral scent. Max wasn't sure whether this was an improvement. He fixed his gaze out the windshield and clamped his lips together. But he could feel Vespa's eyes boring into the side of his head.

The silence stretched.

"Fine," he snapped. "Say it and be done."

"I'm sorry," said Vespa. "I am so, so sorry. My aunt forced me to go undercover in your orphanage—I had no choice."

Max kept staring straight ahead.

"At first," Vespa continued, "it was no problem. I did what she told me, passing tips about your operations. But then, later . . ." She trailed off.

"Later you passed her even more information," said Max. He didn't try to hide his resentment.

"But it was tearing me up," said Vespa, with a catch in her husky voice. "I mean, Hantai Annie welcomed me, made a place for me. And you—you were so kind—"

"—that you told your aunt all about our safe house and gave her what she needed to destroy S.P.I.E.S.," Max interrupted hotly.

She bit her lip. Her eyes radiated hurt.

Belatedly recalling his undercover situation, Max sucked in a deep breath and switched tack. "But I'm not bitter. We're on the same side now, so everything's all tickety-boo. You did what you had to do." His words rang falser than a grade-schooler's fake ID.

Vespa made a strangled sound and plunged her face into her hands. Max sneaked a glimpse, but her tousled blond mane covered everything.

Ebelskeever snorted. "You've got a real way with the ladies, sonny-me-lad."

Max's answering quip died on his lips. He stared out the side window. This game was all too real, its stakes all too high. This was no time for jokes.

◊ ◊ ◊

A half hour later, the gates rolled open and the truck eased down a driveway onto the grounds of LOTUS's headquarters. The house was hidden behind a high brick wall and a fringe of elm trees, although calling it a house would be like calling the Great Wall of China a fence—true as far as it went, but it didn't go nearly far enough.

The sixty-five-room redbrick mansion sprawled arrogantly amid green parkland like a rich, obnoxious guest who couldn't be bothered to leave the party. It boasted a host of bedrooms, enough gables and chimneys for five houses, a tennis court and gym, a dojo, a lab, an underground pistol range, a snake pit, an Olympic-size swimming pool, and a home theater. Max hadn't yet watched a film there, but he supposed that LOTUS screened old James Bond movies and took notes on where the villains went wrong.

The truck pulled up close to the side of the mansion, away from prying eyes. As it stopped, two bulky men hustled out of the house and around the rear of the vehicle. One of them was Albert Styx, formerly of S.P.I.E.S., now with LOTUS— the man who had shot Max's favorite teacher, Mr. Stones. Fortunately, Stones had survived, and was now recovering.

When Styx accidentally caught Max's eye, he nodded curtly. "Segredo."

"Styx," said Max. This was the longest conversation they'd had since he had arrived at the mansion, and that was fine by Max.

With a last glance at Vespa, he slid from the cab and followed Styx and the other agent as they rolled Addison Rook's gurney indoors. She just sat in the truck, watching him.

A pale, grandmotherly woman with a pixie haircut stood in the doorway of one of the side rooms. With her pleasant expression and feathery white hair, she looked as if she might be on the verge of baking them all a batch of gingerbread cookies.

But looks could deceive.

"Take the little brat to the cell," she said as the stretcher trundled past her down the hallway. "And send the parents our ransom demand," continued Mrs. Frost, LOTUS's director.

"Right away, guv'nor," said Styx.

Her storm-gray eyes traveled past Max to Ebelskeever, who was bringing up the rear of the little procession. "So you lost Desmond, did you?"

"We did," the big man replied.

"Sloppy."

At that mild reproach, the burly Ebelskeever seemed to flinch. That alone would've been enough to clue in a stranger to Mrs. Frost's power. "I'll handle it, ma'am," he rumbled.

"I never doubted it." As Max made to follow the others down the hall, Mrs. Frost said, "Young Segredo."

Max stopped. "Yeah?"

"A word in your shell-like ear?" She gestured with one

perfectly manicured hand at the room behind her. It sounded like a request, but Max knew it was a command.

He shrugged a shoulder. "All right."

Max followed her into one of the mansion's numerous sitting rooms. Two built-in bookcases flanked a cheery fire in the brick fireplace. A pair of enormous, sage-colored armchairs and a taupe sofa clustered around a low table. With its silver tea service, Persian rug, and tasteful artwork, the room was the very picture of refinement.

The mansion was everything his shabby old home at Merry Sunshine Orphanage wasn't. Max hated it.

He perched uncomfortably on one of the stiff armchairs and watched as Mrs. Frost poured them each a cup of tea. When the ritual was completed and the cups rested just so on their saucers, she trained her gaze on him.

"And how are you settling in?"

"Well enough," said Max. *Considering that I'm living in a bloody shark tank,* he thought.

"Is everyone treating you nicely?"

"Like a prince," he said. *The prince of darkness.* So far, the LOTUS agents and house staff had welcomed him with responses ranging from suspicion to open hostility.

"Excellent," said Mrs. Frost. "I'm pleased to hear you're finding your place. The atmosphere here can be rather . . . *competitive* at times."

Max snorted a laugh. "Oh, is *that* what you call it when

someone leaves tarantulas in your bed? I was wondering."

Mrs. Frost sipped her tea and inclined her head. "Those rascals. They will test you sometimes."

What was her game? Max wondered. She had tried and finally succeeded in getting him to join her group, but she had to suspect that his true loyalties lay with S.P.I.E.S. and his father, Simon. So why bother recruiting Max for LOTUS?

At the thought of his missing father, Max suppressed a sigh.

After disappearing from Max's life for years, Simon had finally resurfaced, bringing out a host of conflicting feelings in his son. Although he claimed to love Max, the man's loyalties and motives were unclear. He was pro-LOTUS, he was anti-LOTUS. He was protector, betrayer, truth teller, and deceiver, all in one.

Just your typical garden-variety dad, thought Max bitterly.

Mrs. Frost settled her cup into its saucer and leaned toward him. "So far, you've begun playing a small role in our operations, but I believe you have real talent. You're the best natural spy I've seen."

Max made a noncommittal sound. But it was always nice to have your skills acknowledged, even by a mortal enemy.

"We'd like to bring you into the thick of it, give you much more responsibility than Hantai Annie ever did—let you play with all the latest toys and gadgets," Mrs. Frost crooned seductively. "Your potential is enormous, and it was largely wasted at S.P.I.E.S. As I see it, there's no limit to how high you can rise in our organization."

For a heartbeat, Max was a little tempted. He had chafed under Hantai Annie's rules, even though she'd said they were for his own good. He bobbed his head cautiously.

"But before we can invest in developing you into a true superspy," she continued, "we need to see some measure of commitment on your part."

"Commitment?" Was this where they made him take a blood oath and swear his undying loyalty on a sacred wolf skull? Max wondered. "Like what?"

"Something quite easy," said Mrs. Frost. "And for a foster child in your situation, quite necessary, now that Merry Sunshine Orphanage is no more." She lifted a sheaf of papers from the table, selected a stapled document, and handed it to Max.

The heading jumped out at him: PETITION TO ASSUME LEGAL GUARDIANSHIP OF A MINOR. He frowned. "What's this?"

"A simple document. All you need do is write a brief affidavit to the court saying that you want this, and with the stroke of a pen, you demonstrate once and for all where your true loyalties lie." She watched him closely.

A sense of alarm began to penetrate Max's confusion, like the smell of smoke intruding on a deep sleep. "And what happens when I write your statement?"

Mrs. Frost's smile was of the sort found on Bengal tigers just before consuming their prey.

"Why, you become my legal ward, of course," she said.

"Legal . . . ?"

"All neat and tidy, and official," said Mrs. Frost.

"You mean . . . ?"

"Yes, you lucky boy." Her smile widened. "It means I'm adopting you."

CHAPTER 3

CHEESE TEETH
BARS THE WAY

CINNABAR JONES had overslept. Under normal circumstances, that might have meant missing breakfast or being late to class. But these were not normal circumstances.

The sound of voices roused her from her makeshift bed on the break room sofa.

"Wha—?" asked Wyatt, yawning.

"Shh!" Instantly on guard, Cinnabar rolled out from under the coat she'd been using as a blanket and crept to the doorway.

For the past three nights, ever since LOTUS had raided the S.P.I.E.S. safe house, Cinnabar and Wyatt had been living on the run, using their spy skills to break into unguarded buildings at night and sleep in empty offices. The first two mornings, they had left before any workers arrived.

Today, they were not so lucky.

Cinnabar peered out through the doorway into the maze

of cubicles that filled the open-plan office. Fluorescent lights flickered on overhead. A woman's voice said, "And what brings you here so early, Geoff?"

"The bloody Pemberton account," said a man, presumably Geoff.

Stupid, Cinnabar chastised herself. She'd gotten careless, and now she and Wyatt would have to find a way to sneak past these employees.

"Be a love and make us a pot of coffee?" said Geoff.

"It's the twenty-first century," said the woman. "Make it yourself."

Geoff grumbled and a jolt of alarm chased off the last of Cinnabar's sleepiness. *Coffee?* Her gaze swept the break room and landed on the coffeemaker.

Uh-oh.

"Wyatt!" she whispered.

The lump that was Wyatt Jackaroo stirred on its make-shift bed of sofa cushions. "Nngh?"

"Now!" Cinnabar motioned toward the door.

Wyatt sat up, blond hair tousled, blue eyes wide. Like her, he had slept in his clothes, with an overcoat for a blanket.

Cinnabar pointed to her own jacket, and Wyatt snagged it from the couch, tossing it over to her. No sense braving the November chill without protection. Just because Jason Bourne never caught cold didn't mean they wouldn't.

Wyatt joined her at the door. "Why didn't you wake me earlier?" he whispered.

"Why didn't *you* wake *me*?" she shot back.

He blinked. "I was asleep."

Cinnabar rolled her eyes. Honestly, for a techie whiz kid, Wyatt could be awfully thick sometimes. She risked a peek out the doorway.

Seeming to float along the top of the partitions, the head of a handsome, ocher-skinned man was moving their way. They had only seconds to react.

Cinnabar and Wyatt couldn't afford to get caught. The police would surely throw the two orphans back into the foster care system, since nobody at Merry Sunshine Orphanage (the cover for S.P.I.E.S.'s operations) was answering their phone.

And if Cinnabar and Wyatt went back into foster care, they couldn't rescue Max from LOTUS. Not acceptable. Not acceptable at all.

She eyed a gap in the cubicles opposite the doorway. "Let's go," she hissed.

Staying low, they scurried across the passage like rabbits under the shadow of hawk wings. But not fast enough.

"Hey!" the man called. "Who's there?"

"What's wrong?" the woman asked, from another part of the wide room.

Cinnabar and Wyatt hurried down a narrow corridor between dividers, angling toward the office door.

"Two kids," Geoff said. "Must have broken in." His voice

sounded closer. "Come on out now, children. You've got no business being here."

The junior spies reached an intersection in the warren of cubicles.

"This way," whispered Wyatt, pointing straight ahead.

"No, this way," said Cinnabar, pointing left.

A blocky redheaded woman appeared at the end of the corridor straight ahead. "I see them!" she gasped. "They're over here."

Wyatt winced. "How come you're always right?" he muttered.

"Because I'm a girl," said Cinnabar.

They took off running down the left-hand corridor.

"Stop them!" cried the woman. "They're heading for the door."

Cinnabar scanned the scene. The entrance was still another forty feet off, and she could hear Geoff's footsteps pounding away on course to intercept them. Windows lined one side, and a row of offices ringed the other side of this cubicle city.

Time for Plan B.

She ducked into a cubicle.

"You can't hide here!" Wyatt whispered, staggering to a stop. "They'll find us!"

Cinnabar held up her hand in a *wait* gesture. She snatched a stapler off the desk, cocked her arm, and hurled it toward the window side of the room. It landed with a clatter in another cubicle.

"They're over by the windows now!" called the redheaded woman.

"What's the plan?" asked Wyatt, fidgeting. "We've gotta move it like a rat up a rope."

Cinnabar leaned close. "Make for that office," she said, indicating a darkened room in the corner where a door stood ajar.

He gave a nervous nod. Together, they crept away from the cubicle, found a side passage, and hotfooted it toward the office, staying low.

"Anything?" Geoff called.

"Not yet," said the woman. "Block the door so they can't get out."

"Right-o. If I catch the little beggars, then will you make me some coffee?"

Cinnabar could hear the exasperation in the woman's voice. "No, but if you don't catch them, I might splash some on you."

With a quick glance up and down the corridor fronting the offices, Cinnabar and Wyatt darted across it and into the empty room. Ever so gingerly, she eased the door shut, praying that neither of the workers would spot the movement. For once, luck was with her.

"We'll find you wherever you hide." The redhead's call was muffled by the door. "You can't get out."

Cinnabar pivoted away from the door to find Wyatt rummaging through the desk drawers. "Are you mental?" she whispered.

"Nope," said Wyatt. "But I'm hungry enough to eat the southbound end off a northbound horse. And sometimes, these office workers keep . . ." His eyes lit up as he plucked a Kit Kat bar from a drawer. "Ha! Brekkie time!"

Cinnabar shook her head at his thievery and stepped to the window. "Make it a takeaway." She undid the latches and shoved on the pane. It stuck, so she pushed harder.

A blast of November chill gusted through the window as it finally opened. Leaning out, Cinnabar spotted an escape route, along the narrow ledge to the nearest pillar, then down its jutting stone doodads to the ground.

Wyatt joined her at the casement and whistled. "We're lucky."

"How do you figure that?" she said.

"Lucky thing we didn't sleep any later. Lucky thing we didn't pick one of those all-glass office buildings to sleep in. Lucky thing we're only on the second floor."

Cinnabar smirked. "Luck had nothing to do with it, Brekkie Boy."

A short climb and a long walk later, they entered a grimy neighborhood of row houses and shabby little shops. For several blocks now, Cinnabar had had the feeling that they were being followed, but each time she spun around, she spotted nothing out of the ordinary. Paranoia and spies, she thought, shaking her head. Must be an occupational hazard.

She and Wyatt rounded a corner, and the smell of mold, cooked cabbage, and industrial-strength coffee wafted along the street to greet them. The latter aroma came from the building standing before them.

It was an all-night coffee shop, its pink and green neon lights extinguished for the day, and its ancient Egyptian–themed storefront mural faded and peeling in the morning light. The neon tubes above the red door spelled out THE EYE, and in smaller script, ALWAYS OPEN.

Cinnabar's mouth went dry. They were taking a calculated risk by coming here. The café was a hangout for spies of all persuasions, and while she and Wyatt might find the information they sought, they might also attract the attention of someone from LOTUS.

She smoothed back her wiry hair and straightened her shoulders. It was a risk they had to take.

"I dunno," said Wyatt, oblivious. "Looks like a regular coffee shop to me. Common as fleas on a dingo."

Cinnabar lifted an eyebrow. "How long have you been at the School for S.P.I.E.S.?"

"Two years now."

"And you still don't know not to judge based on appearances?"

Wyatt grinned. "Sure I do. For instance, I notice that although you may look smart, you're actually—"

She swatted his arm. "Yuk it up on your own time. These people are serious."

Wyatt seemed abashed, but she knew he wasn't really. Honestly, he and Max were so keen on their little jokes, sometimes you could scarcely have a straight conversation with them.

Gritting her teeth, Cinnabar pushed open the heavy door. She tried to act casual, but visiting The Eye was her last hope for getting a lead on Max's whereabouts. All her other ideas had struck out. If the information broker didn't come through, she wasn't sure what she'd do—except maybe regret that she'd gone after Max instead of rejoining her sister, Jazz.

Instantly, she chided herself. For once, Max needed her more than Jazz did.

They stepped inside. The smell of toast, eggs, and triple-strength espresso was so robust, it was almost a physical thing. It enfolded them with breakfast-y goodness as they stepped through the doorway. But their welcome from the enormous caramel-skinned man wasn't nearly as warm.

"No firearms," he said in a bored growl. His massive body was the size of a small planet, dwarfing the tiny hostess stand and nearly filling the cramped entryway. His small teeth were the yellow of stale cheese.

"We don't have any weapons," said Cinnabar. She held her arms away from her sides for the man's rough pat-down.

Wyatt sent her a sidelong look. "A coffee shop with a bouncer?"

The huge man snorted. "This ain't your granny's coffee shop, grasshopper. Now raise your arms."

Cinnabar said, "We want to talk with Tully."

Cheese Teeth finished frisking them and grunted, "Tully's busy."

"But we—" Cinnabar began.

He hooked a thumb toward the door behind his right shoulder. "Take a seat."

Cinnabar's gaze darted past his other shoulder to the plush burgundy curtain that concealed Tully's office. But nothing short of a squad of marines with flamethrowers and tanks could get past Cheese Teeth—and even then, it would be a close thing. She pursed her lips and edged around him into the coffee shop, with Wyatt trailing behind.

The space was narrow but deep, with a lofty ceiling, colorful wall hangings, and a curved mahogany bar. At this hour, only a handful of the café tables hosted customers, mostly people who seemed like they'd been up all night. Lazy bossa nova music drifted from hidden speakers, transforming the muted conversations into a garbled purr.

Taking a stool at the bar, Cinnabar fished a tiny green change purse from her overcoat pocket. She gnawed her lip. Only a handful of bills remained.

"Enough for a hot cocoa?" asked Wyatt hopefully.

"You know, you could chip in something too," she said.

He spread his palms. "Hey, if I'd known we were gonna

flee for our lives, I would've brought my wallet and a boxed lunch or three. But as it is . . ."

Cinnabar rolled her eyes and ordered them a couple of hot chocolates from the pretty Asian barista. She eyed the menu longingly, but who knew how long their small stash of money would have to last?

Wyatt sneaked glances at the café's other patrons. "Reckon there's any famous spies here?" he asked.

"Sure," said Cinnabar. "That's Mata Hari over in the corner, having tea with James Bond." But she was only half paying attention.

Her thoughts had flown, as they always did, to her older sister, Jazz. It troubled her that for the past two days, nobody had answered the phone at Merry Sunshine Orphanage, where she'd left her sister when they accepted this mission. Cinnabar wanted to catch a train back there and see what was happening, but once again, she rationalized her choice. Jazz had Mr. Stones, Madame Chiffre, and others to take care of her. Max had nobody.

Her jaw tightened like a vise. Nobody besides that skanky bottle blonde, Vespa, who had probably betrayed the entire S.P.I.E.S. operation.

"You all right?" asked Wyatt.

"Never better," she said. "Why?"

His eyebrows lifted. "No reason. Just that you snapped your cinnamon stick like it was somebody's neck."

"If only," she muttered, glancing up into the mirror over the bar.

At a table behind her left shoulder, a hatchet-faced Pakistani man suddenly dropped his gaze and busied himself with his cell phone. Cinnabar frowned. Had the man been watching them?

"Right, then," rumbled a voice from the bottom of a barrel. "Tully will see you now." Cheese Teeth loomed over them, one anaconda-thick arm pointing toward the door.

Cinnabar and Wyatt picked up their mugs and followed The Eye's bouncer back into the cramped entryway. He stood aside and jerked his head at the burgundy curtain. "In you go."

A squadron of butterflies fluttered in Cinnabar's stomach. Taking a calming breath, she brushed aside the velvet hanging and stepped into the lair of the information broker.

HOT SAUSAGES AND KARATE CHOPS

WYATT'S JAW DROPPED. Had he somehow died and gone to heaven without the whole dying part? This was a tech geek's paradise. An entire wall of monitors dominated the room, hooked up to an array of the latest and fastest computers. There were comfy chairs and a sofa, a range of video games, even a mini-fridge.

"Sweet sweetness," he murmured. "When can I move in?"

Cinnabar's sharp elbow poked him in the ribs.

"What?" he said.

The generously curved woman on the sofa chuckled. "Cinnabar Jones, I don't believe I've met your friend."

Wyatt ran a hand over his unruly blond curls. "Wyatt Jackaroo, madam. Love your lair. Absolutely sick."

The woman offered a Mona Lisa smile. "Thanks. I think."

Her walnut-hued cheeks looked creamy enough for

a skin-care ad, and her wise amber eyes twinkled. "I am Roxana Tülay Ochsenfrei. You may call me Tully."

She invited them to sit on the armchairs. Wyatt glanced hungrily at her half-eaten plate of sausages and fried eggs, which rested on the side table. It felt like ages ago that he'd snarfed down that Kit Kat from the office.

"Now, what brings you back here?" Tully asked.

Cinnabar cleared her throat. "Our friend Max Segredo was captured by LOTUS after they attacked our safe house. We're trying to find him."

Tully arched a dark eyebrow. "And you're wondering . . . what? If I can tell you where LOTUS has taken him?"

"Yes, please," said Wyatt. "That, and what happened to Hantai Annie and the rest of our team. If you don't mind."

The information broker wiped at her mouth and shook her head. "You don't want much, do you?"

"Only what's important," said Cinnabar.

"And what's important is costly," said Tully, extending a manicured hand to pull her laptop computer closer. She tapped a few keys. "Let's see . . . I do know something about your team, although my listeners have overheard nothing of Max Segredo's whereabouts, nor of LOTUS HQ's location, for that matter."

Wyatt sagged into the armchair's thick cushions. It had been too much to hope for. Now where would they go for answers?

"However, they did pick up one interesting tidbit about your friend," said the information broker.

"What is it?" Cinnabar half rose from her seat.

Tully raised a finger. "Ah-ah-ah. You know the rules. What will you trade in return?"

Wyatt and Cinnabar exchanged a glance. She had told him that the woman swapped information for money, intel, or favors. Given the sorry state of their finances, money was clearly out of the question. Owing a favor to a stranger sounded a bit dodgy. So that left . . .

"Intel," said Wyatt.

Tully inclined her head. "Go on."

"Um, three nights ago," Wyatt said, "when LOTUS attacked our safe house, they stole a—" Cinnabar's warning glance cut him off. "Stole something very valuable," he finished.

"The electroneuromanipulator?" said Tully. "Old news."

Wyatt gaped. "You know about that?"

"And you can pronounce it?" said Cinnabar.

A dimple appeared in the woman's cheek. "You'd be surprised. Come now, what else can you offer?"

Wyatt stared at Cinnabar. She gnawed her lip.

Tully scooted forward on the sofa. "Do you know, for example, what LOTUS intends to do with this mind-control device?"

Wyatt and Cinnabar shook their heads.

"Pity," said Tully. "Now *that* would be worth something. Government intelligence would pay a pretty penny for . . ." She clacked some keys on her laptop's keyboard and scowled.

"Something wrong?" asked Wyatt.

Tully typed again and cursed under her breath. "This wretched computer. Ever since yesterday, it's been having trouble accessing my VPN."

Wyatt perked up. "Is it your router synching? Or maybe the security encryption protocol?"

She fiddled with her jewelry and raised her eyebrows at him. "This is a highly encrypted, private network—truly state-of-the-art. No offense, but how could a mere boy know what to do?"

Wyatt grinned. "This particular boy has hacked half of the private networks in the country. If I may . . . ?" He reached out for the computer.

With a dubious look, Tully passed it to him. "Very well. But I'm keeping a close eye on you. If you try to hack this, or if you damage anything, Chip will make you rue the day you were born."

"Chip?" he asked.

The information broker cut her eyes toward the doorway, where Cheese Teeth lurked, out of sight.

The corners of Cinnabar's mouth twitched. "That big scary bloke? His name is Chip?"

"Yes," said Tully, eyes narrowing. "Why?"

Cinnabar offered up an innocent expression. "Just curious."

Wyatt, meanwhile, was hard at work diagnosing the computer's problem. A sudden lightness of heart buoyed his spirits. Here, at last, was something he felt equipped to deal with—unlike the task of having to act like a superspy field agent when he wasn't one, or the needle-in-a-haystack challenge of finding his friend Max in a city of some thirteen million souls. As he checked the security protocols, it seemed to him that Tully's MAC address was configured to change every couple of seconds. Could this be causing problems with the network router . . . ?

A growl like a Tasmanian devil in a bad mood rumbled from Wyatt's stomach, breaking his concentration. He glanced up from the screen and eyed Tully's breakfast plate again. "Any chance of a sanger or a sausage?"

"Wyatt," Cinnabar scolded.

The woman didn't blink. "If you can fix that, not only will I tell you what you want to know, but breakfast is on me."

"Wicked!" Wyatt grinned. "A bloke could really get to like this information brokering."

Fifteen minutes later, Wyatt handed the laptop back to Tully Ochsenfrei. "There you go," he said. "It's as flash as a rat with a gold tooth."

Tully raised a quizzical eyebrow, so Wyatt clarified:

"Good as new. And I doubled your processing speed while I was at it."

As he and Cinnabar tucked into their sausage, eggs, and beans with a vengeance, the info broker tested her computer and pronounced herself satisfied.

"We have a deal," she said. "First, I'll tell you what little I know of your team. Victor Vazquez and two or three of your fellow students were spotted yesterday in Chinatown."

"That's a relief," said Wyatt, speaking around a mouthful of sausage. "But what about Hantai Annie?"

The woman shook her head. "Missing."

Silence fell in the information broker's lair as they absorbed the news. Cinnabar was absolutely still. The food caught in Wyatt's throat, and his heartbeat felt sluggish. If all were well, surely Annie would have resurfaced by now?

"And the ones who stayed behind at Merry Sunshine?" asked Cinnabar after a pause. "Any word of them?"

Wyatt knew that Cinnabar's sister, Jazz, was among that crew. When Tully shook her head, Cinnabar chewed a fingernail. Wyatt felt for her. Not having had brothers or sisters, he couldn't imagine what it was like to miss one, but he knew how much he missed his mate Max.

"And now," said Tully briskly, "for the second part of our trade." With a few clicks of the keys, she pulled up a computer file. "One of my sources in the Records Department sent this along late last night."

"What is it?" Cinnabar asked, craning her neck to see.

Tully scanned the document. "Apparently, a Mrs. Helen Frost has taken out a petition to adopt a certain Max Segredo."

"*Adopt?*" spluttered Wyatt, sending sausage bits spraying like a food machine gun.

"But she can't!" cried Cinnabar. "His dad is still alive."

"Apparently it's possible—if the parents can't be found or if the child would be at risk." Tully waved an elegant, plum-nailed hand at the screen. "At any rate, it hasn't been submitted yet, merely initiated."

"But Max would never—he couldn't. I mean . . ." Wyatt said.

Cinnabar set her plate aside. "Come on, Wyatt. We're going."

"What? Where?"

"To find him," she said. "Now."

Wyatt frowned, a bite of egg frozen halfway to his mouth. "But Tully said she doesn't know where Max is."

"Not Max, you cabbage head. *Simon.*" Cinnabar stood. "Tully, where's Simon Segredo?"

The information broker lifted a shoulder. "Somewhere in the city, is all I've heard. And that's all you get from me today."

"Thank you," said Cinnabar. "For everything." She snatched Wyatt's plate off his lap, set it atop her own half-finished meal, and tugged him to his feet. "Move it, slow coach."

"But—" Wyatt snagged one last sausage from his plate as she propelled him toward the curtain.

"Adieu, Wyatt Jackaroo," said Tully with a little finger wave. "If you ever need a job, come look me up."

And that was the last he saw of the information broker, as Cinnabar hustled him through the doorway and out onto the street.

"What's the rush?" he said. "We don't know where Simon is any more than we know where Max is."

Her golden eyes blazed and her fingers dug into his arm. "What's the *rush*? If we don't find Max soon, that old witch will have captured him the legal way, fair and square. We'll never see him again. *Ever*. Do you want that?"

" 'Course not," said Wyatt. "But I don't see how finding Simon Segredo will help."

Cinnabar stopped on the sidewalk and gaped at him. "Duh. The only person who would hate the idea of Max being adopted even more than we do? And Mr. Segredo's a trained agent. If anyone can help us find Max in time, it's him."

They began walking again, edging around a pair of overflowing trash bins at the mouth of an alleyway.

"But you don't trust Max's dad," said Wyatt.

"That doesn't matter now," said Cinnabar. "What matters is stopping Mrs. Frost."

"Excuse me, please," came a voice from behind them. The Pakistani man from the coffee shop stood there with a politely perplexed expression on his face. "Do either of you have the time?"

Up close, Hatchet Face was broad-shouldered and solid, built like the back half of an earthmover. He loomed over them.

Cinnabar took a step back. "Not me."

Out of habit, Wyatt patted the pocket where he usually kept his cell phone, then remembered he'd left it behind when they fled the safe house. "Sorry, mate," he said.

Suddenly a heavy blackjack appeared in Hatchet Face's hand, shielded from the street by his body. "In that case, you will please come with me."

"No, wait—I can guess the time," Wyatt blurted.

He stumbled back a step and glanced around for help. The road was empty. They stood just inside the alley's mouth, with the spy partly blocking them from the sidewalk. Another man, gaunt-cheeked and dead-eyed, emerged from the shadows deeper in the alley. Unhurriedly, he strolled toward them.

"Help us!" cried Cinnabar.

The gaunt man's smile didn't reach his eyes. "That's what I'm doing, pretty girl."

Cinnabar flinched.

"Come along quietly, or I'll be forced to hurt one of you," Hatchet Face said.

"Bugger that," said Wyatt, and he screamed, "Help! Somebody, help!" at the top of his lungs.

The spy spat a curse and advanced on him.

Cinnabar aimed a snap kick at the hand holding the blackjack. Hatchet Face moved at the last second, and the blow glanced off his forearm.

"You'll pay for that, girl!" the man snarled.

Hatchet Face still gripped the lead-weighted weapon, and now he swung viciously at Cinnabar's head, driving her back. She stumbled against one of the bins and went down.

As Hatchet Face pursued Cinnabar, Wyatt whirled to face Dead Eyes, who was stalking him, wielding a wicked-looking knife. Before the man could grab him, Wyatt kicked out at his bony knee. Jackie Chan he wasn't, but he managed to connect with a calf.

Dead Eyes didn't make a sound. He bared his teeth, recovered, and executed a spinning back kick that made Wyatt feel like a woolly mammoth had stomped his chest. He fell to the rough concrete, dazed.

The LOTUS agent stood over him, brandishing the weapon. "When you have a knife, people are supposed to listen to you," he groused, half to himself. "What's wrong with kids today?"

"Poor role models, I presume," said a new voice, like steel wrapped in velvet.

Wyatt blinked.

A third man—tall, lean, and immaculately dressed—now stood behind Dead Eyes. Past him, Hatchet Face lay slumped, unconscious, against a trash bin. Before Dead Eyes could react, the newcomer had karate-chopped his neck and wrenched his knife hand behind his back, causing him to drop the weapon.

As the LOTUS agent struggled, the tall man calmly drew a yellow-and-black Taser from his trench-coat pocket and zapped him at point-blank range. The man sank to the ground, twitching like a landed flounder.

"I—uh, oh. Wow," said Wyatt.

"You're welcome," said Simon Segredo.

CHAPTER 5

THE ENGLISH MUFFIN GAMBIT

IF ANY ROOM in the LOTUS mansion was likely to contain valuable secrets, like the location of Max's friends, it was the comfortable study that served as Mrs. Frost's office. As far as Max could tell, there were only two problems with accessing those secrets: one, finding a time when the LOTUS chief would be away from her office; and two, breaking into the blasted place.

During his brief time at the mansion, Max had wandered every hall, every open room, checking the security measures as inconspicuously as possible. The office presented a challenge. Two cameras covered the hallway outside it, and the door boasted a biometric, keypad-controlled lock. Plus, three guards randomly patrolled the house at all hours, so you never knew when they might come down that corridor.

The ceilings were solid, so you couldn't break in from above, the windows were barred, and the heating vents were too narrow to accommodate a person, even one as slim as Max. Not so much as a cockroach could sneak in undetected.

No, as far as Max could tell, the office security had only one weak link: the bathroom. A chance remark from the butler, Leathers, had revealed that the study shared a bathroom with the neighboring second-floor room.

Vespa's bedroom.

Now the only problem was how to sneak through the bedroom of someone he hated, in order to break into the office of someone he despised. Yep, life here at LOTUS was all just unicorns and rainbows, Max reflected. What a family.

Speaking of families, he'd managed to delay writing Mrs. Frost's adoption statement, claiming that he needed time to think before making such a major decision. The move had bought him a day or two, but the calculating scrutiny in the woman's icy eyes told Max that this delay came with an expiration date.

He planned to be long gone by then.

And when it came to fleeing, Max really didn't want to leave LOTUS HQ empty-handed. He couldn't head blindly off into the city; he needed some line on where to find his friends—maybe even his missing father.

And if he could steal a couple of secrets that might hurt or hinder LOTUS, so much the better.

The opportunity to snoop arrived sooner than he'd anticipated, at dinner that same night. The meal took place in the enormous formal dining room, a chamber dripping with crystal chandeliers, gilt mirrors, and all manner of fussy antique furniture. Despite that clutter, the room was still large enough to accommodate an entire family of waltzing elephants, a symphony orchestra, and an aardvark.

Max sat with Vespa, Mrs. Frost, and her assistant, a man named Bozzini, at a table designed to hold thirty. Servers, including the crusty old butler Leathers, bustled in and out bearing platters and tureens. Given all the fuss, it could've been a state dinner for diplomats, rather than a casual evening at home with murderous friends and family.

It was so different from the chaotic camaraderie of dinners at Merry Sunshine Orphanage. People laughing, arguing, the dog begging for food, Tremaine throwing dinner rolls to Rashid. *That* was a family meal. With a pang as sharp as a blade, Max missed Hantai Annie Wong. Her gruff manner concealed a huge heart—unlike Mrs. Frost, whose polite demeanor concealed a heart the size of a pomegranate seed.

Working his way through a slice of apricot-stuffed lamb shoulder, Max monitored Mrs. Frost's conversation. Unsurprisingly, it was all about work.

"They've agreed to your demand," said Bozzini, reading from his computer tablet. He was a lipless, olive-skinned man with all the sparkle, humor, and excitability of a bowl of lukewarm linguine.

"Excellent," said Mrs. Frost. "And when will it be ready?"

"Mr. Rook says"—Bozzini consulted the tablet again—"tomorrow afternoon."

Max's ears perked up at the mention of the mind-control device's inventor, Addison's father.

"He's weak and sentimental," Mrs. Frost said, patting her lips with a linen napkin. "I knew our little ploy would work."

The sweet lamb turned bitter in his mouth and Max swallowed uncomfortably. Caring about a kidnapped son made someone weak? Mrs. Frost had about as much maternal feeling as a hammerhead shark.

"Have a team standing by to make the trade."

The assistant inclined his head. "Already done, ma'am."

Mrs. Frost's lips pursed in a tiny smile. "Such efficiency."

"I live to serve."

Max glanced up from his plate to find Vespa mouthing "I live to serve" behind her napkin. She rolled her eyes at her aunt's exchange, and Max suppressed a snort of laughter. He had to remind himself that he loathed her.

Still, this tidbit was news. LOTUS would possess a working mind-control device by tomorrow night, and the S.P.I.E.S. team needed to know about it. Perhaps while snooping for his friends' location, Max might uncover LOTUS's intentions. Which made it all the more important for Max to get a look inside that office and—

"You're finished?" asked a voice from behind. Max started, then glanced up to find a young woman, part Asian like himself, with her hand extended.

He nodded. The server cleared away the lamb and replaced it with a plate of asparagus in vinaigrette sauce. Oh, yum.

"Don't you like asparagus?" asked Mrs. Frost.

"Love it," he said. "Nearly as much as brussels sprouts and haggis, combined."

Max was just starting to puzzle over how he could get Vespa and Mrs. Frost out of the house at the same time. Start a fire? Flood the bathrooms? Invent a shoe sale? Then he finally caught a break.

"Vespa, dear," said the woman, "don't forget our little errand after dinner. Time to pick up our new pet."

With a smirk, Max wondered whether that pet would be a pit viper or a piranha. His money was on the piranha.

"Do I have to go?" Vespa asked.

Mrs. Frost's lips thinned into a white slash. "You know better than to waste my time with such questions."

The blond girl sighed. "Yes, Auntie. I'll be ready."

Max kept his gaze down, focused on cutting his asparagus. How perfect. And he didn't even need to set anything ablaze.

An hour later, Max sat in his third-floor bedroom, pretending to read a book, with his back to the surveillance camera hidden in his alarm clock. When he'd first discovered the camera, he considered destroying it, but then he realized it was better to have surveillance you knew about than surveillance you didn't.

Either way, Max knew he was living under a microscope, and he was good and sick of it.

The purr of a car engine caught his attention. He rose and peeked out the window. Illuminated by a floodlight, Mrs. Frost and Vespa were crossing the gravel below toward an idling Mercedes SUV with a trailer hooked to the back. Max revised his guess about the pet from piranha to alligator. Did LOTUS buy nothing but high-end luxury cars, he wondered, or had Mrs. Frost worked out some sort of endorsement deal? He could almost see the ad: *The automotive choice of evil spies for over thirty years.*

He waited until the vehicle had motored off, then pocketed a couple of useful items and headed out the bedroom door. The hallway was quiet, the ivory carpeting as deep and plush as God's own bathrobe.

Making his way to the edge of the staircase, Max stopped and listened to determine if the coast was clear. He'd brought along a handheld video game as a cover, and as he waited, he started to play.

A good thing he did too. Because no sooner had he booted up a game than Humphrey Wall's close-cropped brown dome appeared below him, rising as the man climbed the steps. When he saw Max, he stopped abruptly.

"Oi, what you doing?" said the agent, his hand resting on the butt of a pistol at his waist.

"Dancing the hoochie-koo with the Queen Mum," said Max. "What's it look like?"

Humphrey's legs spread wide, and his lip curled. "Don't push me, boy."

"Or what? You'll shoot me for playing a video game?" said Max.

"You don't wanna know what I'd do." His voice was as hard and flat as stale peanut brittle.

Max feigned a yawn. "You're right," he said. "I don't."

"Hmph." The agent glared at him a moment longer, seething. Then, since playing *Grand Theft Auto* wasn't on his list of approved reasons for killing someone, Humphrey brushed past and swaggered off down the hallway, growling, "Keep your nose clean."

"Sure. Got a hankie?"

Max silently released his held breath. Keeping up the bored-teenager act, he ambled casually down the stairs. He knew that the mansion bristled with more cameras than the red carpet on Oscars night, and that his movements were likely being recorded. Heart hammering, he proceeded to the first floor. What he needed was a mild distraction—nothing too extreme—for Humphrey and the other roaming security guards.

His feet found their way down to the kitchen. Pausing in the doorway, Max scanned the gleaming, oak-floored room, packed with enough Sub-Zero freezers, groaning pantries, and high-tech culinary equipment to supply a dozen reality-show cooking competitions. His gaze traveled down the counter and landed on a toaster that looked like it could control a space shuttle mission.

Hmm . . .

Max smiled. A burned English muffin, a blaring smoke alarm, and voilà—instant distraction.

He dug the bread out of the pantry, cranked the toaster setting to nuclear fusion level, and popped in the muffin. Shielding his next move with his body, Max then nudged the food processor's handle over to hold the toaster's lever down.

A woman's voice spoke. "Still hungry?"

Max nearly jumped out of his skin. With a superhuman effort at casualness, he turned, still blocking the rigged toaster with his body. "Er, yes. I've never been keen on eating lamb. Bad for the environment, you know."

"What, do lambs pollute?"

It was the part-Asian server from dinner, bearing an empty glass and a plate with the remains of her own meal.

"Pollute? Er, no," said Max. "It's, um, the global footprint?" He had no clue what he was talking about.

"Cattle are bigger than lambs," said the woman. "Wouldn't they leave bigger footprints, then?" A wry smile played at her lips as she scraped her leftovers into the garbage disposal.

"Er . . ."

The silence stretched like the waistband of some ancient gym shorts. Max fidgeted while she flipped the disposal's switch and wiped the glossy countertop with a dish towel, his mind focused on the rigged toaster behind him. Did he smell burned toast already?

"I've got a high metabolism as well," said Max. "I scoff food like I've got a hollow stomach." Then, realizing how foolish that sounded, he forced a laugh and added, "Um, I guess we all do. Otherwise the food would have no place to go."

The server glanced up at him with a look that said, *Who is this git?* No wry smile this time.

More long seconds ticked by. Finally, she finished up and turned to go. Max offered a breezy "Great talk—see you around, then" as the woman headed out the door shaking her head.

He waited as long as he dared, making sure she was truly gone. The burned-toast smell intensified.

Then he sauntered out of the kitchen, tapping away at his video game and whistling under his breath. By the time the distant blare of the smoke alarm began, he was just reaching the second floor. Max dodged into the nearest open room and waited until he heard footsteps clomping down the stairs.

From here, Max knew, he would need to be particularly sneaky. He fished a laser pointer from his pocket and switched it on, holding the object atop the game player. Then he strolled into the corridor, angling the device so that it pointed up at the juncture where the ceiling met the wall— where the surveillance cameras clung.

Max kept his face angled downward over the game, but his eyes up. When he rounded the corner into the stretch of hallway where Mrs. Frost's study lay, he made sure to give both cameras a full blast of infrared laser pointer.

They didn't beep or emit smoke or do anything to indicate that they were disabled. Still, Max trusted crafty Mr. Stones, who had taught him this trick. He pocketed the pointer and worked the doorknob, slipping into Vespa's darkened bedroom.

The scent of tropical flowers, strong and sweet, enveloped him—Vespa's scent. It reminded him of her smooth skin, her toffee-brown eyes, her tumble of blond hair . . . Max shook his head. Why was he thinking of this now? With an effort, he concentrated on the task at hand.

Like a beacon, the golden glow of a night-light guided him into the bathroom. No cameras here, as far as he could tell. Max had to trust that Mrs. Frost wouldn't let the guards spy on her own niece in the loo. He tried the door that connected to Mrs. Frost's office.

Locked, of course. He pulled out his picks and went to work.

After five minutes of dedicated effort, the knob turned and the door swung open. His stomach flipped like a trained seal. Moving lightly on the balls of his feet, Max made his way into the heart of LOTUS's operations, Mrs. Frost's inner sanctum.

CHAPTER 6

HIDE AND CREEP

AS EVIL HEADQUARTERS WENT, Mrs. Frost's was right up there with the best of them—if your idea of evil headquarters was a posh accountant's office. The broad maple desk held a high-end computer, a green-shaded lamp, a sleek telephone, a nearly empty in-box, and a pair of crouching lion statuettes carved in onyx. The bookshelves bulged with scads of leather-bound volumes that simply screamed "technical and boring." Cherry-colored embers glowed in the fireplace.

All in all, it looked less like the sort of place where you'd hire an assassin, and more like the sort of place where your rich uncle Cedric would get his taxes done.

But Max knew that the office, like Mrs. Frost herself, hid its true nature beneath a sophisticated veneer. He sifted through the reports in the in-box. Nothing relevant. His gaze snagged on a flyer for some kind of circus, and he thought,

Does Mrs. Frost have a thing for clowns? He tried to log on to the computer. Password protected. Not for the first time, Max wished that he possessed Wyatt's techno skills—or that he could just pick up the computer and shake it until all the secrets spilled out.

He prowled the room, snooping behind books and paintings. Nothing—not even a cobweb. Max gritted his teeth. No filing cabinets graced the tidy chamber, no handy maps highlighted his friends' whereabouts. The desk itself had only two drawers—one containing stationery, and the other office supplies. Not so much as a camera pen or an eraser bomb to be seen.

Max clasped his hands on top of his head and pivoted slowly, surveying the room. What was he missing? This was it, the nerve center of LOTUS's operations, the heart of its evil domain. So why wasn't there more . . . evil spy stuff?

On an impulse, he reached out and lifted one of the lion statues, hoping to uncover a secret stash, microfilm taped to its bottom—anything, really. What happened next made up for all his frustration.

For the statue didn't lift; it folded back on a hinge. And when it did, something creaked behind him. Max spun to see a whole section of the floor slide away into the baseboard, revealing a spiral staircase that trailed down into dimness.

Hairs stood up on the back of his neck and his breath came faster.

"Now that's more like it," he muttered. Pulling a tiny LED flashlight from his jeans, he flicked it on and descended the steps. When his head was level with the floor, Max hesitated. Should he leave the passageway open like this? What if someone should visit the office above while he was exploring down below?

Then his light picked out a switch on the center post of the stairs, several steps lower. When Max flipped it, the floor slid back into place above him. LOTUS, it seemed, had very courteously thought of everything.

He continued along the metal steps, following the cone of illumination thrown by his flashlight. As he proceeded down and down, below what must've been the ground floor, the thought struck him: What, they couldn't afford elevators? But before long, the tight cylinder of the staircase opened into a wider space, and he had reached the bottom.

Splashing his light about the place, Max gave a low whistle. Now, *this* was an evil lair to end all evil lairs.

Brushed-steel floors stretched farther than his beam could reach. Rows of open-fronted lockers to his left contained an array of weapons and espionage equipment impressive enough to make the Pentagon revise its Christmas list. Max saw all manner of rifles and pistols, as well as nets, Kevlar vests, ninja throwing stars, laser weapons, grenade launchers, flashbangs, and devices he couldn't begin to puzzle out. One locker even held what appeared to be a personal jet pack.

On an elevated sort of command center to his right, Max noticed several swivel chairs fronting a bank of controls, lit by the cool azure glow of the massive computer screens above them. On one screen, he recognized an electronic map of the capital decorated with blinking dots of various colors. Could these be his missing friends and father? Max hustled over to the screen and peered up at it, heart splashing in his chest. Although most of the dots were motionless, a few crawled along what Max guessed were motorways. He scanned the display. Where was a handy-dandy caption, something to give meaning to these random spots of color?

Nowhere, that's where.

He leaned over the controls, pondering how to coax more information from this mysterious machine. Spotting an ENTER button, he pressed it.

Instantly, the map vanished.

"No!" burst from Max's lips. *Whoops.* His hand flew to his mouth, and he shone the flashlight around, making sure he was still alone, that no one had overheard.

The chamber was as deserted as an ice cream shop in the dead of winter.

He turned his attention back to the screen, which now displayed a list of names, most of which had the word *minister* before them. Where had the map gone? Max tapped the ENTER key again, and now the layout of an extensive building appeared. One more tap, and it zoomed in.

A section bearing labels like CENTRAL LOBBY and HOUSE OF COMMONS filled the screen. The Houses of Parliament? He frowned. Was LOTUS planning on infiltrating the government?

Before he could investigate further, a familiar sound sent a jolt of adrenaline coursing through his body.

A sustained creak up above. Voices.

Someone was coming down the stairs!

Max whipped his flashlight about in a wide arc, searching for a hiding place. The rows of lockers offered scant protection. Ditto for the command center. But in the wall beyond it, two corridors opened into deeper darkness.

He hustled across and plunged into the right-hand hallway. Shielding his beam now, Max tiptoed down the narrow passage past doors guarded by card-scanner locks. When he judged he'd gone far enough, he hugged the wall, clicked off his light, and listened.

Footsteps clattered on the steel steps.

"I tell you, it ain't necessary." Humphrey's gruff voice grew louder as he descended.

"The guv'nor decides what's necessary," snapped a sharp female voice. Dijon LeStrange. "And she wants security double tight."

Max tensed. *The guv'nor* meant Mrs. Frost. Was she home already?

Lights snapped on, and Max had to squint against the sudden brightness.

"See?" said Humphrey, his words echoing in the cavernous room. "Nobody home."

"That's your whole inspection?" Disapproval drenched Dijon's tone like curry on rice. "Good thing you're not on gate duty. The enemy could roll a bloody Trojan horse past you."

"Get knotted," said Humphrey. "I just don't fancy wasting effort, that's all."

At the end of his passage, back the way he'd come, Max could see a slice of the larger chamber. If either of the guards walked past, they would be able to see him too, plain as day. He glanced behind him, searching for a safer spot. A stack of cardboard boxes rested near the corridor's dead end. Perfect.

"Ooh, listen to Mr. Efficiency," sneered Dijon. "'Wasted effort,' he says. For your information, if the cameras malfunction, it's not a waste of time to check and see if any bad guys are about."

Creeping back to his hiding spot, Max thought, *Bad guys? They're* the bad guys. He ducked into place and winced as his knee bumped a box.

"What was that?" said Dijon.

Max froze.

"The prisoner, no doubt," said Humphrey.

"Come on, then," said Dijon. "Let's go look. Unless you fancy finding other employment."

Humphrey grumbled. Max hugged the wall as the footsteps drew closer, and now he could see the agents through a narrow gap—Humphrey, buff and broad-shouldered; Dijon, sinister and svelte. They stopped at the first door. The grumpy spy drew his weapon, and Dijon slid a key card through the scanner.

As soon as the door opened, a high, anxious voice emerged. "Don't hurt me! What do you want? My parents are rich; they'll give you whatever you want. Just don't hurt me, please!"

Addison Rook.

With all that had happened since, Max had nearly forgotten about the boy genius he'd helped kidnap only that morning. Now he felt a twinge of sympathy for the twit. Nobody deserved to be kidnapped and imprisoned, not even Addison. But since the teen was a valuable pawn, Max knew he wouldn't be harmed. He scowled and pushed the thought from his mind. Addison just wasn't his problem.

And if that made him heartless, well, secret agents and foster kids didn't survive by being as gooey as a box of Christmas chocolates.

"Don't wet your bloody pants, boy," growled Humphrey. "We're only checking up on you."

"Oh." Addison's relief was almost comical.

"Are the accommodations to your liking?" asked Dijon with a sarcastic lilt. "Is the food up to snuff?"

"The cell is . . . adequate," said Addison, a hint of his self-assurance creeping back. "The lamb, though, was a tad overdone."

Humphrey snarled and took a step closer.

"But I like it that way?" the boy genius squeaked, his voice jumping an octave.

Dijon shut the door, and the electronic lock clicked.

"*Now* can we go?" Humphrey groused. "The guv'nor will be home any minute."

"All right, then." She led the way back into the main room, her voice receding. "But I want you to go check on that brat Segredo, make sure he's not up to mischief."

Uh-oh.

Max squeezed his eyes shut. He wouldn't be able to take his time and try to locate his friends on that blasted computer. Instead, he'd have to sneak back upstairs, pray he didn't get caught, and devise a reasonable excuse to cover his time spent snooping.

The overhead lights snapped off, and the guards' footsteps retreated up the stairs. When Max heard the false floor slide back into place, he snapped on his flashlight and recrossed the evil lair. Moving as cautiously as a long-tailed cat in a roomful of rocking chairs, he scaled the staircase, careful not to make a sound. At the top, Max put an ear to the false floor, listening for any sign of human activity. Nothing. Only a faint electrical hum.

Max reached down and flipped the switch. As the floor above him began to retract, he rushed up the last steps and into Mrs. Frost's office. If someone *was* waiting, he at least wanted to meet them head-on.

The chamber lay empty. A quiet pop came from the fireplace as the sap in one of the logs ignited. Max released a breath he didn't know he'd been holding.

So far, so good.

He worked the lion statuette, and the floor slid back into place. Taking one last glance at the office, he made his way to the bathroom door, passed through, and relocked it.

When he spun around, Max nearly jumped out of his skin.

"What in the world," said Vespa, "are you doing in my loo?"

DOING THE DEAD DROP

HER CONVERSATION with Simon Segredo wasn't going quite the way Cinnabar had hoped.

"You're both certifiably brainsick," said Mr. Segredo. "You think you can waltz into LOTUS headquarters, just the two of you, and rescue Max? From the best-guarded, most secure spy compound in the country?"

"Not just the two of us," said Wyatt. "We were hoping you'd come too."

Max's father only raised his eyebrows in response. He paced the dingy parlor of the cut-rate hotel suite he'd taken them to, peering out between rust-colored curtains at the gloomy day outside.

In spite of the man's impeccable pearl-gray suit, Cinnabar thought Mr. Segredo looked haggard. His cheeks were hollow, his brown eyes shadowed with fatigue. Maybe he wasn't trustworthy, but he *was* Max's dad. He deserved to know. . . .

"We haven't told you everything," said Cinnabar.

Mr. Segredo wheeled back toward her, his long face impassive. "All right."

Cinnabar and Wyatt traded a glance. "It's Mrs. Frost," Wyatt began.

"She's trying to adopt Max," Cinnabar finished.

Mr. Segredo's jaw tightened, but that was the only sign of whatever he was feeling. "Adopt him. And you know this how?"

"Tully has a source," said Cinnabar.

The tall spy rubbed a hand across his face.

"We can't let it happen," said Wyatt. "Obviously."

"I see." Mr. Segredo seemed lost in thought.

"Don't you care?" Cinnabar rocketed up off the ratty sofa and crossed to him. "Look, I don't trust you, seeing as how you've worked for LOTUS—"

"Understandable," said Max's father.

"But no matter what, Max is your son," said Cinnabar. "How could you let him be adopted by that evil old bat?"

Simon Segredo massaged the back of his neck, his gaze troubled.

"It's not Max, it's me," he said.

"Really?" asked Wyatt. "She's trying to adopt you too?"

Max's father shook his head. "She's trying to hit me where I'm most vulnerable."

"So hit back," Cinnabar pleaded. "Help us find LOTUS's new headquarters and rescue Max."

"This is my concern, not yours," said Mr. Segredo. "I've got something they want, so it's best if I sort this out on my own. You kids shouldn't get involved."

Cinnabar's temper flared. "Well, pardon me for living, but it's not your decision. We're *already* involved."

Wyatt stood to join her. "She's right. Max is our mate, and we won't abandon him, no matter which ruthless granny has got her mitts on him."

Mr. Segredo crossed his arms and looked from one of them to the other for a few heartbeats, eyes narrowed. Finally, he nodded to himself. "Max is lucky to have friends like you."

"So . . . ?" Cinnabar's gaze searched his face.

"So, I'm glad there's someone who knows where LOTUS headquarters is."

Cinnabar frowned. "Who?"

"Me."

Cinnabar felt completely gobsmacked. For the first time in a long while, she couldn't speak.

Wyatt gasped. "You *know*? Stuff a duck, you mean you've known all this time?"

"Yes," said Max's father.

Cinnabar's hand flew to her heart. "But why? If you know where he is, why haven't you already rescued Max?"

Turning away, Mr. Segredo drew in a long breath and blew it out. "It's not as simple as you think."

"Sure it is." She followed him, heat rising to her face. "You go in, you get him, you bring him out. Done."

"Easy-peasy," said Wyatt.

The tall spy grimaced. "For one thing, I've been splitting my time between watching LOTUS and watching you."

"Us?" Cinnabar rocked back on her heels. "Why us?"

"You're Max's closest friends. If anything happened to you, he'd never forgive me. *I'd* never forgive me."

She brushed aside his explanation. "Forget us—worry about him. We can take care of ourselves."

Mr. Segredo's smile was a sardonic one. "Like you were doing outside The Eye?"

Cinnabar flushed and studied the carpet. She had no comeback.

"And what's the other thing?" said Wyatt.

"Sorry?"

The blond boy scratched his cheek. "You said, 'for one thing.' What's the other?"

"I need a solid plan, based on trustworthy intel—which I've almost got." Max's father faced them squarely. "And I need a team."

Wyatt made a voilà gesture that took in himself and Cinnabar. "Presto change-o, here we are."

"No offense, but for a compound that well protected,

I need a team that's a bit more . . . substantial," said Mr. Segredo. "You mentioned one of your teachers and his crew were in Chinatown?"

Cinnabar's brow crinkled. "Mr. Vazquez? But Tully only said they'd been spotted. We don't have an address, or even a phone number."

Mr. Segredo tut-tutted. "What do they teach you young spies these days? Didn't your crew ever work out a dead-drop system or another way of passing messages?"

Wyatt's eyes lit up. He snapped his fingers. "Gumtree! Of course."

"Gumtree?" said Cinnabar. "Is that some Australian thing?"

"Tell you in a sec," said Wyatt. "All we need's a computer."

Max's father produced a compact laptop model from his duffel bag. "Here. Get going on that while I work on round-ing up some resources."

Hours later, as daylight bled from the room, Cinnabar rose from the sofa and stretched a crick out of her back. Scribbled plans littered the cheap coffee table, and Wyatt hunched over the laptop computer like a vulture over roadkill.

"How about now?" she asked him.

He sighed. "For the twelve hundred and thirteenth time, Cinn, I'll get an e-mail alert when someone responds."

One half of a muted conversation drifted from behind the

closed bedroom door. Cinnabar glanced over at it. Who was Mr. Segredo calling? she wondered. He'd been absolutely smashing when he saved them from the LOTUS agents, but her suspicion was a habit that died hard. Would they be able to trust him when the chips were down?

The electronic chime of the computer jolted her from her reverie. Cinnabar strode back to the sofa. "Well?"

Wyatt opened the e-mail message. So far, their few responses to the online classified ad for an "exotic pet" on Gumtree.com had all come from normal people. Cinnabar was beginning to wonder whether the rest of the S.P.I.E.S. team had forgotten that long-ago class on passing coded messages online.

Then a grin split Wyatt's face. "Bonzer!" he whooped.

"It's them?"

"Mr. V wants to know where he can meet us and get a gander at our bunyip."

"That's brilliant!" Cinnabar quirked an eyebrow. "Um, bunyip?"

Wyatt smirked. "It's an Aussie thing. You wouldn't understand."

Cinnabar sank onto the couch beside him. "So where do we meet?"

At that moment, the bedroom door swung open, and Simon Segredo strode into the room, wiping his hands on a sky-blue silk handkerchief.

"And?" asked Wyatt.

"Success," said Mr. Segredo, as calm and relaxed as if he'd just returned from a day at the spa.

"How did you manage to find what we needed?" Cinnabar asked.

"I traded favors with some, shall we say, less than savory acquaintances."

Cinnabar stiffened, unable to hide her reaction.

"My dear Cinnabar," said Mr. Segredo. "Unlike your precious Hantai Annie, I am willing to do whatever needs to be done." He tucked the handkerchief into his breast pocket and brushed some invisible lint off his lapels. "Now, any luck reaching Vazquez?"

Wyatt flashed two thumbs up. "All we need is a meeting place."

"Excellent." Max's father pulled a small notebook from a jacket pocket, scribbled on it, and passed the note to Wyatt. "Here's the spot. Tell them eight o'clock."

Cinnabar felt a sudden lightness in her chest. This day was certainly ending on a much more positive note than it had begun on. With the team about to reunite, they finally stood a chance of rescuing Max before he was lost to them forever. Who knew? This harebrained mission might actually work out after all.

ᕯ ᕯ ᕯ

"Seriously? Here?" said Cinnabar. "Of all the places in the city, you wanted to meet here, right in the middle of all this?"

She stood with Wyatt and Mr. Segredo on a crowded sidewalk in the heart of the capital, across from the famous square that was one of its most popular tourist attractions.

Even at night, the neighborhood crackled with energy. Pods of American retirees, clusters of German teens, and small knots of Chinese tour groups formed the boulders in the stream of humanity that flowed up the street. When the stoplight changed, Mr. Segredo led Cinnabar and Wyatt across, into the wide square with its spotlighted fountains and towering monolith. The fumes from fleets of cars, red double-deckers, and tour buses made the place smell like an oversize petrol station.

"You've gotta admit," said Wyatt, "there aren't many meeting places more public than this."

"That's the whole idea," said Mr. Segredo, guiding them around a chattering group of Italians and up to a railing that overlooked the square. "The more public, the less likely that LOTUS will try something."

"But how would they even know we're meeting here?" asked Cinnabar.

An ironic smile crossed Mr. Segredo's face. "Aside from the fact that your organization has more holes in it than Swiss cheese? Let me put it this way: You know which spies live to a ripe old age?"

"Which ones?" asked Wyatt.

"The paranoid ones," said Max's father, opening his gear bag. "You two check for your friends. I'll watch for any watchers. Here." He tucked some objects into their jacket pockets. "A few useful items, just in case."

Cinnabar patted the comforting weight in her pocket. She gazed out over the cloverleaf-shaped fountains, glowing ice blue in the darkness, at the statue of the old war hero on his high column, and at the figures winding in and out of shadows between them. She scanned for familiar profiles and recognizable gestures amid the press of strangers. And then . . .

"There!" Cinnabar pointed at a cluster of people by one of the lion sculptures at the monument's base.

Wyatt leaned forward, squinting. "Is that Tremaine? And Mr. Vazquez?" He whirled back. "Hey, Mr. Segredo, look at—"

But Simon Segredo had melted away into the night.

"Who is he," said Wyatt, "Batman?"

"Come on!" Cinnabar snatched at his sleeve, hurrying over to the steps. She and Wyatt descended steadily, watching the small group across the square. Mr. Vazquez glanced her way, and Cinnabar was surprised at the catch in her throat.

After several days of living on the run, she hadn't realized how much she'd missed being with her own people.

Cinnabar half stumbled, breaking into a sprint as they got closer.

Mr. V pointed at her, saying something as three other heads swung her way: Rashid, Tremaine, and Nikki Knucks. All three grinned, even Nikki, and then Cinnabar found herself swept up in Tremaine's warm, licorice-scented embrace.

"Give a brother a hug!" cried the teak-skinned boy.

The next few moments were a whirl of embraces and back thumping and overlapping greetings. When Cinnabar and Wyatt stood back from their fellow orphans, Mr. Vazquez was finally able to slip in a coherent word.

"My friends," he said, "I am so very glad to see you. We feared the worst."

"We experienced the worst," said Wyatt. "Try surviving on Twix and stale break-room biscuits for a couple days."

"Not like you couldn't stand to drop a few pounds," Nikki teased, poking his belly.

For once, her taunts didn't rattle Wyatt. "Aw, I missed you too, Nikki," he said mock-sweetly, drawing hoots from the two older boys. Nikki blushed to match her red hair and scowled like an Easter Island statue.

"Where have you been?" asked solemn Rashid.

"Hunting for Max," said Cinnabar. "LOTUS captured him after the raid."

Tremaine winced. He could usually be counted on for a joke and a smile, but now his face wore a troubled expression.

"Hantai Annie is missing, and Miss Moorthy, too," he said. "Dunno what became of Mr. Dobasch. Sad days, sister."

"So let's go get them all back," said Cinnabar. "Starting with Max."

Mr. V nodded. "Let's do it."

Her mouth fell open. "Really? Just like that?"

"Of course."

"But . . ." She frowned. "I thought you'd try to talk us out of such a dangerous mission."

"Normally, I would." Mr. V's handsome face, more like a tango instructor's than a computer expert's, seemed drawn and tired. "But you don't know the whole story."

Wyatt and Cinnabar traded a look. "What do you mean?" asked Wyatt.

"While we were out stealing the mind-control thing-umabob," said Tremaine bitterly, "LOTUS was busy burning down Merry Sunshine Orphanage."

"*What?!*" cried Cinnabar and Wyatt together.

An iron fist crushed Cinnabar's heart. She had trouble catching a breath. "My sister!" She grabbed Mr. Vazquez's arm. "What happened to Jazz?"

"And Mr. Stones?" asked Wyatt. "The other kids?"

The teacher patted her shoulder. "Don't worry. Mr. Stones and Madame Chiffre got everyone out in time. They sent a message—they're hiding out somewhere safe."

Cinnabar reeled. Her sister was safe, and Merry Sunshine

was . . . gone. A strange cocktail of relief, regret, and cold rage surged through her veins. Jaw clenched, she snarled, "They'll pay. Those ratbags won't get away with it."

"Ratbags?" said a familiar voice. Cinnabar spun to see the massive bulk of the traitor Alfred Styx looming over her. He smiled a sharklike smile. "Now is that any way to talk about an old friend?"

THE SHORT END
OF THE STYX

WYATT GAPED. The last time he'd seen Styx, the big man had been chasing them down a hall at LOTUS HQ, brandishing an assault rifle. Now here he stood, larger than life, wrapped in a navy-blue trench coat and sporting a crew cut so sharp it could shave the ink off a newspaper. Wyatt stepped back, instantly on the alert.

"Tired of the tucker at LOTUS?" he asked nervously. "Looking to rejoin your old mates?"

"After I was so well treated at S.P.I.E.S.?" Styx made a sour grin, like someone who bites down on a chocolate truffle only to discover earwax inside. "Not bloody likely," he growled. He swiveled his blocky head to the left and whistled sharply between his teeth.

At the signal, four LOTUS agents in dark suits materialized as if conjured by a magician, encircling the orphans and their teacher.

Styx plunged a meaty paw into his overcoat pocket, poking the object inside against the fabric and pointing it at Cinnabar. As Mr. V made a move toward his own weapon, the big man said, "Ah-ah-ah. Think twice, Vazquez. Hantai Annie would never forgive you for making me spill orphans' blood."

Cinnabar blanched, and the other kids froze. Wyatt's heart hammered like a thrash-metal drum solo.

Mr. V's eyes narrowed. "You wouldn't."

"You don't know what I'd do," rasped Styx. "And neither do I. So let's not find out."

Wyatt glanced left and right. Now would be a really bonzer time for Simon Segredo to make an appearance. But the dapper spy was nowhere in sight.

"How'd you find us?" asked Cinnabar.

Styx snorted. "Think you're the only one who remembers the old procedures? I've been checking the 'Pets for Sale' section of that Web site ever since we took down your safe house. Hacking your e-mails was child's play."

"Let the children go," said Mr. Vazquez. "I'll come along quietly."

Styx shook his thick head. "Mrs. Frost wouldn't approve."

"She doesn't let you think for yourself?" Wyatt asked, half surprised at his own audacity. "Got you on a pretty tight leash, then?"

Styx's face clenched like a fist. "The old witch doesn't appreciate what she has. But she will."

"Aww, you're not feeling the love?" Nikki needled him.

"Seems that happens a lot with you, eh, Styxie?" Wyatt said. He wasn't sure why, but keeping Styx annoyed and distracted seemed like a good strategy.

The big man snarled like a rabid grizzly bear. *"Enough!"* Wyatt flinched, rethinking his strategy.

"You, don't call me Styxie," the enormous spy snapped, jabbing a finger at Wyatt. His glare swept over the rest of the group. "You lot, come with us. March!"

Wyatt, torn between fear and bravado, caught Cinnabar's eye. She glanced at his pocket and gave him the tiniest of nods, reminding him of the useful items that Mr. Segredo had slipped them. He nodded back.

Cinnabar folded her arms. "And what if we won't go with you? Would you really shoot down a bunch of unarmed orphans in public?"

"Don't push him," said Rashid. "I don't want to know."

Styx clamped one of his huge hands around Cinnabar's arm. His pale face was mottled with anger, like a bruised apple. "Button your lip, missy. Or I'll button it for you."

A female LOTUS agent stepped up beside him, looking like a Rottweiler in a pantsuit. "The car's waiting," she said, indicating the gray Mercedes van idling at the edge of the square despite angry honks from other vehicles. "Let's not have a scene."

Styx grunted. He yanked Cinnabar along as he trundled

toward the van, and the other LOTUS spies herded the group of teens.

"No, by all means," Cinnabar said, her voice growing louder, "let's have a scene. Let's have one right *now!*"

And with that, she tugged Mr. Segredo's bulky yellow-and-black pistol from her overcoat and Tased Styx in the spot where a man would least like to be Tased.

"Wooaugh!" With a wordless cry, the huge spy folded at the waist and crumpled to the pavement, twitching and jerking.

Wyatt pulled his hands from his pockets, brandishing a smoke bomb in each. "Mind your eyes!" he cried to his fellow orphans.

Foomf! Billows of bluish smoke engulfed the group as the bombs hit the pavement. Nearby tourists shouted in alarm and scrambled away.

"Fire!" Wyatt yelled, fanning their panic. "Run!"

"Follow me!" cried Cinnabar.

Between the sulfurous smoke and the tears in his eyes, Wyatt had trouble telling one blurry figure from the next, but he found Nikki and shoved her toward Cinnabar. When he went to search for Rashid, Rottweiler Woman seized his arm in a death grip.

"Gotcha!" she snarled. "You rotten little—"

Wyatt whipped a canister of pepper spray from his overcoat, spritzing it right into whatever insult waited on the tip of her tongue. Down went Rottweiler Woman, coughing and gagging. He stumbled after Cinnabar and Nikki, pushing past the freaked-out tourists and another incapacitated LOTUS spy.

A gunshot barked in the confusion, and someone cried out.

Once past the smoke cloud, Wyatt spotted Mr. Vazquez supporting a wounded Rashid, hustling along one edge of the square. The rest of the orphans were just ahead of them. Wyatt hurried to catch up.

Then he noticed the Mercedes van gliding along the curb behind them, like a tiger shark trailing a school of fish.

"Look out!" he cried.

Cinnabar and Tremaine glanced back, dismay etched across their faces. They picked up the pace, but the vehicle was closing the gap.

The van's curbside window was down. Wyatt swatted at his coat pockets, fumbling for another smoke bomb . . . there! He wasn't the world's greatest cricket player—okay, possibly the world's worst—so he'd have to get close.

Sprinting toward the van, he managed to work the grenade free. Over the hubbub in the square, it sounded like the shadowy driver was shouting something. Wyatt cocked his arm.

At that moment, a stray beam of streetlight caught the man's face—the thin lips, the long jaw. Simon Segredo! And just as the grenade left Wyatt's hand, he heard Max's father's words: "Get in the van, you moppets!"

An hour later, after a chilly ride with all the windows down and multiple apologies from Wyatt, they returned to Mr. Vazquez's Chinatown hideout to regroup. Along the way, they dropped Rashid at the hospital. His shoulder wound was painful but not critical, and Mr. V promised to come back soon to stay with him.

The teens and the two adults spread out in the living room of the shabby flat over the Soon Fatt restaurant. Time to enjoy their takeout meal and see whether the eatery lived up to its name.

"This is—mmmf—*so* yummo," Wyatt mumbled, assaulting a plateful of lemon chicken-y bliss. He felt like he hadn't had a decent meal in donkey's years.

"Keep your hands and arms well back, ladies and gents," said Nikki. "The rare Tasmanian warthog has been known to munch stray fingers."

"Ha-ha," said Wyatt. But with his full mouth, it sounded more like "hng-hng."

Mr. Segredo wiped his lips on a napkin. "First things first. Before we begin this reckless and possibly suicidal mission, we'll need all the help we can get. Where's the rest of your group?"

Mr. V set down his chopsticks. "Stones, Madame Chiffre,

and the other students are back in our town, not far from the orphanage—or what's left of it." He grimaced.

"And how many are reliable operatives?"

Mr. Vazquez gave an expressive shrug. "Stones, for certain. Chiffre, Catarina . . . maybe Jazz."

"If my sister's up for it," said Cinnabar. Her expression put the issue in serious doubt. Wyatt knew Jazz was still dealing with the psychological aftereffects of being imprisoned by LOTUS. He shuddered in sympathy.

Max's father rose and began to pace the long room—just like Max did when he was working through something, Wyatt noticed. "We'll need to scout the place more thoroughly," Mr. Segredo mused. "Maybe Stones can cover for you while you're with Rashid. What about Hantai Annie?"

Mr. Vazquez shook his head. "In the wind. I can't raise her on mobile phone or any of our other contact methods. I'm afraid . . ."

The teens' chopsticks slowed to a halt, an even truer sign of their emotional state than the glum expressions on their faces.

"She's out there somewhere," said Wyatt staunchly. "Takes more than a little midnight raid to knock our Annie out of the action." But his optimism was as hollow as a lead pipe and the chicken felt like a gluey lump in his gut.

Max's father glanced out the window at the neon-tinged night, then turned to the group. He clasped his hands behind his back like a general surveying his troops. "So what are our assets?"

Mr. Vazquez made a wry face. "A couple of weapons, that laptop"—he indicated the computer on a side table—"and the clothes on our back. You?"

"My deadly wit, a gear bag full of all the goodies I could muster, and my trusty Beretta," said Max's father. "If Stones joins us, we've got six agents, four of them kids. That's on our side of the equation."

"And on the other side?" Wyatt asked.

"The latest security equipment, oodles of cash, enough weapons to arm several militias, squadrons of crack agents, and total ruthlessness—in short, all the might and majesty of LOTUS in their own stronghold."

"Cho!" Tremaine chuckled. "Frost won't stand a chance, mon."

CHAPTER 9

LOO
CONFESSIONS

MAX'S HEART threatened to pound its way out of his chest like a Rock'em Sock'em Robot. He froze, pinned in place by Vespa's stare.

"What are you doing in my toilet?" she said, standing in the doorway to her bathroom. One hand rested on her sweater-clad chest and her eyes were wide, though she didn't seem scared, merely surprised.

"I, er," Max said. Involuntarily, he glanced back the way he'd come, at the door that led to Mrs. Frost's office, then caught himself.

Vespa's lips parted. "You went in *there?*" she breathed.

As Max saw it, he had two choices: lie like a broken watch and hope she believed it, or tell the truth and hope she didn't expose him. Given their history, he chose the lie.

"I had to talk," Max said, feigning embarrassment. "I, er, felt bad about how I've been treating you, so I came in here to wait, and—"

She arched an eyebrow. "To wait in my loo?"

"Er, no. In your bedroom. And then I . . ."

Vespa cocked her head. "Have you stalked many girls?"

Max blushed and looked away. "No. Never."

"Sneaking into someone's bedroom when they're away? Stalker move," she said, the ghost of a smile playing about her lips. "I won't say I'm not flattered, but . . ."

Vespa stepped in so close, Max could feel her breath on his face. He noticed flecks of gold in her brown eyes, and in a rush of guilty feeling, that gold reminded him of Cinnabar's eyes.

"Uh," he said. His cheeks felt warm.

"You and I both know the truth," she whispered.

"We—" Max's voice broke. "We do?"

She nodded, and Max felt like he was standing in a garden, the smell of flowers was so strong. "You broke into my aunt's office to spy on her," she breathed.

"That's ridic—" His denial died off when Vespa laid her index finger on his lips. He'd never met a girl who did that before.

"Shh," she whispered. "My room is bugged. If we whisper, they'll just think we're having an intimate conversation. In my bedroom."

Max's cheeks grew warm. "I—I'm not spying on your aunt," he whispered, trying to stay focused.

"For a good spy, you're a terrible liar," said Vespa. "But don't worry, I'll keep your secret."

Max stared into those big brown eyes. A whirlpool of feelings coursed through him—doubt, hope, worry, relief, and something else he couldn't put a name to.

"Max, I'm your friend."

"Friends don't betray each other," he spat, before he could stop himself.

She winced. "They don't. What happened before won't happen again. I promise."

Max's lips pursed. Could he really trust her? At this point, he had no choice but to pretend he could. He nodded.

A relieved smile lit her face like sudden sunshine. "Good. Now play along with me. I don't know if she's got cameras in my room, but I know there's a bug or two."

"Okay," said Max.

"You're so fresh!" Vespa's voice grew louder and she assumed a flirty tone. "I can't believe you said that."

Max followed her back into the bedroom. He tried for a suave attitude. "Believe it, baby."

They both grimaced at his clumsy attempt to be Joe Smooth.

But Vespa kept up their cover. She giggled. "That's enough out of you! Better scoot before my aunt finds out."

"Later, then," said Max, reaching for the knob. With the door half-open, he veered back to make some parting comment. But the impact of two warm lips on his cheek left him stunned.

"For the cameras," Vespa murmured.

"Uh," said Max. And he stumbled from the room into the hallway.

"*There* you are," said Humphrey, rounding the corner. His gaze flicked over Max's shoulder, then back to his face, and he grinned wolfishly. "Lover boy."

Max looked around. Vespa was shutting the door, and she blew him a kiss.

"That's me," said Max. "Lover boy."

Humphrey shook his head, chuckling. "The guv'nor won't be pleased when she hears of your shenanigans."

"Don't tell?" Max pleaded.

"Boy," said the agent, "ain't no secrets in this place."

Max crossed and uncrossed his arms, thinking of what he'd actually been up to. For the sake of his mission and his life, he sincerely hoped Humphrey's statement wasn't true.

Later that night, as he tossed and turned, waiting for sleep, all Max could think of was escaping from LOTUS by any means necessary. (Well, that, and the touch of Vespa's lips on his cheek.) Maybe he was disappointing Hantai Annie by not continuing as a double agent, but he just couldn't—not with the threat of Mrs. Frost's adoption hanging over him. No, he had to escape at the first opportunity.

He'd take one more stab at searching the hidden command center for information on his friends' whereabouts, and if that failed, well, he'd simply have to bolt. Maybe Max could avoid cops, LOTUS, and truant officers long enough to find his friends and warn them that LOTUS was plotting against the government. Maybe not. But at least he wouldn't be sitting around on his behind, waiting for the ax to fall.

That decision made, he drifted at last into an uneasy slumber.

At breakfast the next morning, Max toyed with his eggs and toast. The part of his mind that wasn't worrying about Vespa—and wondering about that kiss—brimmed with escape plans and ploys for revisiting the secret chamber. At the same time, he also speculated on what beef LOTUS's chief had with the government. Tax problems? Passed over for some high honor?

So lost in thought was he that Max jerked when he realized Mrs. Frost was addressing him.

"Er, how's that?" he asked.

"I said," Mrs. Frost repeated tartly, "what did you get up to last night?"

"Up to?" Max suppressed a guilty cringe. "Not much," he said. "Playing video games, snacking, plotting world domination. The usual." He carefully avoided Vespa's gaze.

"Really?" said LOTUS's chief with mock innocence. "A little bird told me you had romance on your mind."

Max could feel his ears getting warm. There truly *were* no secrets in this house. "Your bird was confused," he said. "I, er . . ."

The spymaster chuckled. "Can't say as I blame you. She is lovely, my niece." Now Vespa blushed and stared at her plate. "But we do have certain standards to uphold in this family. There will be no hanky-panky under this roof, do I make myself clear?"

"Auntie!" said Vespa. "We would never—"

"See to it that you don't, my girl," said Mrs. Frost. The white-haired woman leveled her penetrating gaze on Max. "Now then, have you reached a decision about our new . . . living arrangement?"

Bozzini and Vespa both shifted to watch him. Max clenched a hand on his leg under the table. This would require some finesse.

"Not yet," he said carefully. "I . . . feel so honored that you're willing to give me a permanent home. There's nothing I want more," he said, with perfect sincerity.

"But?" Those gray eyes pinned him in place like a moth on a corkboard.

Max focused on cutting a bite of his fried eggs. "Well . . . I'd feel better about it—more complete—if I knew what happened to Hantai Annie, Wyatt, and the rest." He managed a shrug. "Easier to let go, and all that."

He chewed slowly, wondering if Mrs. Frost might actually let slip the info he needed.

"Dead," she said, her voice as unemotional as if she were describing the weather.

Max nearly choked on his egg. He'd worried, of course, but never in his worst imaginings had he believed them to be gone.

"They're dead to you," said the spymaster. "No matter where they are. If you're truly to become one of us, no more attachments to anyone in your old life."

A roaring filled his ears. With an effort, Max kept his fists from shaking. How *dare* she toy with him like that. "Not even my dad?" he asked, throat tight.

"Your *father*." Mrs. Frost's voice was as cold as a year's worth of Januarys. "After he abandoned you for so long, after he caused your mother's death—still you hold out hope? Your father," she said, beheading a sausage, "is no one's idea of a father."

Although he wanted to slap the woman for her cruelty and stand up for his dad, something inside Max withered at her words. The truth stung. Yes, Simon Segredo had disappeared when Max was little more than a toddler, only to resurface last month. And yes, in their few encounters since then, he had lied, manipulated, and persuaded Max to betray his friends. Not exactly Father of the Year material. But still . . .

"I need more time," said Max. "This is a big decision."

Mrs. Frost tore a scone in half with a twist of her wrist. "I am a patient woman. But I will not have my generosity taken for granted. You shall give me an answer by tonight. Understood?"

Max nodded, afraid to trust his voice. *Tonight?* This called for drastic measures. He wolfed down the rest of his breakfast, but then the tureen of porridge caught his eye, and a sudden inspiration struck.

Picking up his plate and cutlery, Max said. "Delicious. Think I'll go pay my compliments to the chef." But as he rose, Mrs. Frost wagged her fork in admonishment.

"Now, now. Where are your manners? Did you ask to be excused?"

Max rolled his eyes. "Can I be excused?"

"It's 'may I,' and yes, you may," said the grandmotherly spymaster. "I can see you'll require quite a lot of training in manners and grammar."

All the more reason to duck this adoption, thought Max. He offered a phony smile and took his leave. Pushing through the swinging door, he entered the warm bustle of the kitchen, with its homey smells of toast and sausage and lemony soap.

The part-Asian server was setting out the staff's breakfasts on a sturdy oak table by the windows while the second server, a skinny brunette, rinsed cooking utensils and loaded them into a dishwasher.

Lovingly scrubbing a skillet at the sink stood a middle-aged woman with salt-and-pepper hair, skin like polished ebony, and a thick, sturdy frame wrapped in an apron. The cook, Max guessed.

He passed his plate to the brunette and addressed the woman at the sink. "My compliments," he said. "First-rate breakfast."

Her smile was as broad as her Scottish brogue. "Thank ye, laddie. Not many here bother to say thanks—save Mrs. Frost, of course. Impeccable manners, that woman."

For a heartless killer, Max thought. Aloud, he added, "I was wondering, does everyone in the house eat the same food?"

"Oh, aye," said the cook. "Save for the really fancy dishes. That's front room only."

Max cocked his head. "Really? So the guards, for example, will have the same lunch as me today?"

"The smoked haddock chowder? Aye, they will." She rinsed off the pan. "Why do ye ask?"

"No reason." Max lifted a shoulder. "Just wanting everyone to enjoy the same lovely meals as me." Inwardly, he cringed. Would the cook buy this bald flattery?

She beamed as she dried the skillet. "Sweet lad. If only the rest of this crew were half as thoughtful."

If only you knew, thought Max. But all he said was, "You're too kind."

WYNKEN, BLYNKEN, AND GNAWED

AFTER A SESSION of Internet research on one of the mansion's computers, Max carefully deleted his browsing history. He might not be the most tech-savvy kid around, but he did know that a good spy always covers his tracks. With a bit of snooping through a bathroom cabinet, he located the necessary ingredients, and then decided he'd better scout out his escape route.

Heading downstairs and along the main hall, Max ambled up to the back door and tried it. Locked. And what's worse, it was controlled by a key card—and thus completely invulnerable to his lock picks. Max noted that the windows were locked also, and wired with alarms. LOTUS must not be too keen on getting fresh air.

He was about to go case all the possible exits, when a cheerful whistling caught his attention. Down the hallway trundled the Scottish cook, carrying a teal-blue overcoat and a purse large enough to hold several baked hams, a butter churn, and a bucket of gravy.

"Ah," said Max. "Mrs., er . . ."

"Cheeseworthy," the woman said. "I'm off to do me shopping. Are ye going somewhere?"

Max made a face. "Well, I was planning to stroll around the grounds, but"—he slapped his pockets—"I seem to have left my card upstairs. So forgetful."

Mrs. Cheeseworthy's glance went from Max to the door. Her brow furrowed, and he could almost hear her thinking, *Is this kid a guest or a captive?*

"I'll just slip out with you," said Max, patting her arm. "It'll be all right."

"Well, if you're sure . . ."

He offered his most trustworthy smile. "It's not like I'm a prisoner. Mrs. Frost *is* planning to adopt me, after all."

"Oh, aye?" said the cook. Her moonlike face still reflected doubt.

"It's a walk around heavily protected grounds," said Max, forcing a chuckle. "What could happen?"

"That's true." Mrs. Cheeseworthy's expression softened. "Ye seem a nice enough sort. I don't mind saving ye the trip upstairs."

"Thanks, ma'am." Max tried to hide a triumphant grin. He couldn't believe how easy this was. For a LOTUS employee, the cook was pretty trusting.

"And of course, if ye try any mischief," she said, "ye'll be savaged by dogs or shot by guards."

Max felt his jaw drop. "Uh, of course."

Mrs. Cheeseworthy beamed, slid her card through the scanner, and the lock clicked open.

Recovering himself and opening the door with a flourish, Max said, "After you." He even helped the cook into her overcoat, like the world's last surviving gentleman.

With a finger wave, Mrs. Cheeseworthy crunched across the gravel to an ancient Volvo parked far away from the gleaming Mercedes and BMWs, as if the luxury cars were embarrassed to be seen in its company. Max jammed his hands into his jeans pockets and sauntered across the parking area. To an observer, he was merely a kid stretching his legs after being cooped up all morning.

But his eyes roved constantly, noting details. The gardener and her assistant, trimming a hedge. The chauffeur polishing a Bentley, shoulder holster bulging under his jacket. The cameras mounted on light posts.

Giving the workers a friendly wave, he stepped down into the garden, which was larger than an average city's public park. Ranks of rosebushes stretched off in either direction, pruned back for winter. Fantastic hedges carved into lions and tigers and wolves lined the top of a gentle slope, overlooking enough green rolling lawns to make Tiger Woods drool.

Making his way around an ornamental fountain bristling

with cherubs and nymphs, Max headed for the thick stand of trees that bordered the lawn. They were tall enough, he noted, to easily conceal the LOTUS estate from its neighbors.

Just before he reached the little grove, Max noticed a long, low building tucked away in the bottommost area of the grounds. Unlike the rest of the structures, it was charmless, concrete, and blocky, and when the wind blew from that direction, he caught a whiff of ripeness—something like wet straw and dog poop. The kennels, maybe? If so, Mrs. Frost must keep enough dogs to stage her own private Iditarod race, he thought. Or maybe that was where they had stashed last night's mystery pet.

It was cooler among the trees, and when Max pushed aside a branch, it sprinkled him with moisture from the rain earlier that morning. The grove stood tall, but not so deep, and soon he passed through it, fetching up against the brick wall that surrounded the property.

And what a wall.

The barrier stood a dozen feet high and was topped with two strands of razor wire—most likely electrified, Max guessed. All tree branches were trimmed far enough back that not even a howler monkey on steroids could make the leap over the wall without hitting the wire.

Max rubbed his forehead. As far as he knew, his family tree had a distinct lack of circus acrobats. There must be another way out. . . .

He walked a short distance along the path that ringed the perimeter. Kicking at the dirt, he wondered whether he might be able to dig a tunnel of some sort, and then he saw it: seven letters scratched into the damp soil.

Squatting for a closer inspection, Max made out: *G-A-M-B-A-R-E*. "Game-bear?" he muttered, sounding it out. Clearly, the message had been inscribed this morning, after the rain. Was it encoded? And if so, who was it meant for?

His train of thought was derailed when a savage barking erupted behind him.

"Oi!" came a rough voice. "Where you think you're going?"

It was Styx, the turncoat S.P.I.E.S. agent, being pulled along by two massive, black-and-tan Rottweilers. The huge man wore a scowl like it was the latest Paris fashion. His glare was hot enough to throw sparks.

"Don't have a thrombo," said Max. He rose and casually smeared the letters with his foot as he wheeled about. "I'm only stretching my legs."

Styx stopped about eight feet away. Like iron filings in the presence of a magnet, the dogs pulled to the end of their leashes, eyes glued to Max, growling continuously.

"Stretching your sodding legs?" Styx snarled. "What's this look like, a bloody park?"

Max took in all the manicured trees, the brick wall, and the impeccably groomed path between them. "Well," he said, "yes."

"Har-bloody-har," said the hulking spy. "No outdoor privileges for you. Boss lady said so."

"She's afraid the sun will damage my delicate skin?" said Max.

"She's afraid you'll hop the wall and sell us out to the highest bidder," said Styx.

Max acted offended. "You mean she doesn't trust me? I'm wounded."

"Keep up the comedy, and my mates Wynken and Blynken will show you what wounded really means."

Max eyed the nearer dog. Its lips had peeled back from a seriously sharp set of fangs, and a rope of drool dangled from its chops. The growling continued unabated, like a pack of Hell's Angels revving their choppers.

Lifting his hands in mock surrender, Max let Styx and his canine companions herd him back toward the mansion. As they crossed the lawn, he asked the big man, "So, how's your new employer working out?"

"None of your business," said Styx.

"They giving you loads more responsibility? Respecting your mad skills?"

Styx said nothing. His face was like a shuttered shop window on New Year's Day.

"No, then?" said Max as they skirted the fountain. "Don't take it too hard, mate. Mrs. Frost hasn't exactly handed me the keys to the kingdom either—not like Hantai Annie did."

Styx grunted, eyes narrowing.

Mentioning Annie's name triggered something in Max. It reminded him of the way she used to tell him to hang in there—or *gambare*, in her fractured Japanese English. Wait, *gambare*? What if the letters G-A-M-B-A-R-E weren't *game-bear*, but a message from Hantai Annie herself? Had she somehow made it over the wall? Was she even now—

A dog snarled. "Oi," said Styx, prodding Max. "Pick up your feet, Segredo."

Max came back to himself, discovering he'd stopped dead. He couldn't let Styx know what he suspected. What on earth had they just been talking about? Oh, right.

"Maybe Mrs. Frost doesn't give us responsibility because she's afraid we'll betray her to S.P.I.E.S.," he said, trying to keep his face neutral.

The massive man snorted. "Nothing left to betray her to. My team nearly rounded up Vazquez with some of the last dregs."

Max's stomach gave a flutter at the mention of his friends. Although starved for word of them, he kept his gaze on the mansion and maintained a casual tone. "Oh, yeah? Nearly?"

"Your blasted girlfriend got in the way."

Max turned a chuckle into a cough. "That's a shame."

"Wait till I catch up with her," the big spy snarled. "I'll teach her not to mess with Styx."

With a rush of protective feeling toward Cinnabar, Max's

next words came out sharper than he'd intended. "Sounds like *they* taught *you* a thing or two. Everyone got away, eh?"

They crunched across the gravel, the dogs herding Max up to the mansion's side entrance.

"Not for long," said Styx. He fed his key card into the reader, and the door clicked open. "We got teams out searching. A handful of kids and a lone techie? They're sitting ducks."

Styx worked the doorknob and gave Max a none-too-gentle shove into the house. "Stay inside," he rumbled. "Next time, I unleash the dogs."

As if they'd picked up on the threat, Wynken and Blynken rumbled a parting growl, their amber eyes glaring daggers at Max.

"Something to look forward to," he said, shutting the door in their furry faces.

Max drew a long breath and blew it out, a floating sensation spreading through him. Was Annie really on the grounds somewhere? And if so, should he proceed with his escape plan or start hunting for her? Lost in thought, he wandered down the hall until a slender figure blocked his path.

"You," said Dijon. "You think you're so smart."

"Me?" said Max. "A little above average, maybe."

She leaned closer, hands fisted on hips. Her black eyes drilled into him. "Well, I know what you're up to, little man."

"Really?" said Max. A chill rippled through him, but he

kept up a bland front. "I wish you'd tell me. I rarely know what I'm up to."

"Nobody believes you've come over, not even the guv'nor." A cold smile appeared on her lovely face. "I've got my eye on you, and when you slip up . . ." Dijon snapped her fingers.

"You'll click your fingers at me?" said Max.

"I'll break your neck like a breadstick," said Dijon, and she sauntered off down the hall as if she owned the whole darned place.

Such lovely people here, thought Max. Can't imagine why I'd want to leave.

WALKING THE MOP

CHAPTER 11

CINNABAR'S BUTT felt deader than a zombie's conscience, deader than disco, deader than Julius Caesar's pet goldfish. She'd been sitting in the crowded backseat of the nondescript van for what seemed like days, but was only hours. Her back was stiff, the stale air smelled of body odor and bean farts; she was cold, crabby, and beginning to be seriously cheesed off at Nikki.

But none of that mattered.

Well, not much, anyway. Because they were parked down the street from LOTUS HQ, where Max was being held captive, and because tonight, they would rush in and save his narrow behind from a fate worse than death.

She elbowed Wyatt, sitting beside her. "What's happening now?"

"Still nothing," he said, continuing to monitor the side

rearview mirror. "Same as when you asked five minutes ago. Crikey, you're a broken record."

"Well, I can't see anything, can I?"

On her other side, Nikki snorted. "Should've thought of that before you chose your seat, Skinnybar."

Cinnabar ground her teeth. She hated when Nikki was right—not that it happened very often. "Mr. Segredo, let's at least go check out the perimeter?"

"Soon." Max's father shifted in the driver's seat, never taking his eyes off the small hand mirror that reflected the mansion's front gate.

Cinnabar blew out a sigh. She was a patient person by nature, but this endless surveillance was wearing on her last nerve. "Why not now?"

Mr. Segredo half swiveled and pointed out the window. "See that post on the wall?"

"Yes."

"Notice the camera up top? They've got eyes on the sidewalk."

"So?" said Nikki.

"So," said Mr. Segredo, "they know some of us by sight. If we just stroll down the street, they'll recognize us in a heartbeat, scoop us up, and then where would Max be?"

"Where he belongs," Nikki muttered.

Cinnabar dug an elbow between Nikki's ribs, and Max's father shot the redhead a sharp look.

"If you'd rather be somewhere else, Miss Knucks, I suggest you go there," he said. "This is risky enough even with everyone fully committed."

Nikki nudged Cinnabar back, but then she wilted under Mr. Segredo's stare. "I'm good," she mumbled.

"Tremaine," Max's father said, turning to the athletic teen beside him. "You ready for your part?"

Tremaine grinned, giving him a thumbs-up. "All aces, mon." He was dressed in a black hoodie and baggy jeans, giving him the appearance of a typical hip-hop-loving college kid.

"Nikki?"

Similarly attired, Nikki grunted, "Yup."

Mr. Segredo watched a delivery truck rumble along the road. "Use the lorry for cover, and . . . go!"

As soon as the truck passed between their van and the camera, Nikki and Tremaine hopped out, hurrying toward sections of the wall about a hundred feet apart. Each pulled a can of purple spray paint from their hoodie pocket and began plastering the redbrick wall with colorful graffiti.

"Not that I don't love seeing LOTUS get tagged," said Wyatt. "But how exactly will this help us rescue Max?"

"Watch and learn," said Mr. Segredo, his eyes on the gate.

A whine came from the van's cargo space, and Cinnabar reached back to pat the head of their borrowed pet, a scraggly brown mutt that looked like a cross between an Irish wolfhound, a badger, and a mop. "Easy there, girl. You'll get your walkies soon."

"She's not the only one who needs to have a hey-diddle-diddle," said Wyatt, crossing his legs.

"I told you to use the loo before we left," said Cinnabar. "Honestly, you—"

"Focus!" snapped Mr. Segredo.

Cinnabar scooted into Nikki's spot, and she and Wyatt watched the rearview mirrors. Outside, Tremaine and Nikki were still spraying graffiti, the Jamaican teen adding some green highlights to his purple EAT THE RICH tag. At last, the gate cranked open, and a chubby man in a peacoat and balaclava rushed out.

"Oi!" he cried. "You're in for it now, you little beggars!"

"There," said Simon Segredo, checking his watch. "Nearly five minutes."

Nikki and Tremaine disappeared down the street in opposite directions, running like a pair of cheetahs who'd been drinking from an espresso pool. The guard wasn't nearly so fleet. After a halfhearted chase, he shook his fist at Nikki and stomped back to the gate out of breath, barking a complaint into his walkie-talkie.

"A small revenge, but sweet," said Wyatt.

"And what did we learn?" asked Mr. Segredo.

Cinnabar narrowed her eyes thoughtfully. "They don't have their A Team on security."

Max's father nodded. "And why?"

"Five minutes is a pretty slow response time," she said.
"And?"

"That guard wasn't exactly young Arnold Schwarzenegger,"
said Wyatt. "He couldn't even catch Nikki, and he was pant-
ing like a sunstruck dingo."

"Very good," said Simon Segredo. "And from that we can
deduce . . . ?"

Cinnabar and Wyatt swapped a glance. "Um, LOTUS
guards need more cardio training?" she said.

Mr. Segredo quirked an eyebrow. "LOTUS," he said, "is
using their best agents for something else."

Wyatt grinned. "Leaving the castle undefended?"

"Hardly. It'll still be a tough nut to crack. But at least
we've got the ghost of a chance."

Cinnabar rolled her eyes. "Such confidence. I feel *so* much
better."

Max's father started up the van and pulled away from
the curb. "Let's go collect your friends and test another part
of the perimeter."

"There are loads of words to describe Nikki," said
Cinnabar. "But 'friend' isn't the first one I'd pick."

The vehicle made its way down the road and around the
corner, where Tremaine and Nikki were waiting. They piled
in, and Mr. Segredo took them onto a street that wound
around to a block of homes on the other side of the mansion.

Stopping before another grand house, Max's father said, "I happen to know this family is away on holiday. Wyatt, Cinnabar, let's suit up."

Cinnabar stuffed her wiry hair under a loose newsboy cap and slipped on a pair of sunglasses while Wyatt disguised his appearance with a baseball cap and an oversize raincoat.

"Whatever you do," said Mr. Segredo, "don't stare directly into any cameras. A LOTUS guard might recognize you from the time you visited their former HQ, and the last thing we want to do is tip our hand."

"Roger that," said Wyatt.

"'Roger that,'" mocked Nikki. "Can't you just say 'okay,' like a regular person?"

Wyatt sent her a dirty look, but said nothing as he picked up the dog's leash and stepped from the van.

"Anything specific you want to know?" Cinnabar asked Mr. Segredo.

He ticked the points off on his fingers. "Number of cameras, any blind spots, and anyplace where the wall is vulnerable."

"No worries," said Cinnabar. But that wasn't strictly true. Inside, she had enough worries for the whole crew and then some. How would they get in, how would they find Max, had he succumbed to Vespa's charms yet, and, oh yeah, how the heck would they escape from the high-security compound right under LOTUS's noses?

But "Back in a flash" was all she said.

When she rounded the side of the van, Wyatt had already attached the leash to the shaggy dog's collar. "What's its name again?" she asked.

"Ziggy," said Wyatt, trying to pet the creature as it ducked away from his caresses. "And he's such a gooood boy, idn't he, oodgie-woodge-ums?" This last bit was crooned at the dog.

Honestly, thought Cinn, why do people treat animals like babies? "She's a girl, cabbage head. If you're done getting all smoochy-woochy, let's go."

Wyatt lugged the four-legged mop out of the van and onto the sidewalk, the dog struggling with him all the way. "Just trying to bond," he said. "We're meant to be his owners, after all."

Cinnabar smirked. "Only a blind man would take that for your dog."

"I'm more of a cat person." Wyatt sighed.

Keeping an eye on the windows in case Mr. Segredo had been misinformed about the homeowners, they crossed the lawn, making for the side of the house. Ziggy dragged Wyatt back and forth across the grass like a deranged speedboat towing a water skier. Finally, the blond boy managed to tug the beast onto a neat series of stepping-stones that led under overhanging trees and around to the back.

Here, they wound between ornamental hedges, potted shrubs, and lawn furniture to the back of the property, where it ended at the brick wall that encircled LOTUS HQ.

Someone had cleared about five feet of land in a ring around the wall, thus creating the perfect path for walking the dog.

Mindful of Simon Segredo's warning, both Cinnabar and Wyatt kept their faces averted from the high mounted cameras. As they strolled from one yard to the next, Cinnabar kept cutting her eyes at the top of the wall.

"Looks like they've got at least five cameras, spaced about thirty feet apart," she muttered to Wyatt. "Think we could short one of them out?"

"In a jiffy," he said, "but they'd probably send someone to investigate. What we need is . . ." He gaped at a sturdy plane tree whose thick branches hung close to the wall.

"What?" said Cinnabar, when he stayed mute.

"What, what?" Wyatt blinked at her.

She gave an exasperated snort. "What do we need? You said we need something."

"Oh, *that* what." A sneaky smile spread across his face. "We need an innocent-looking way of creating the short. And I might have just found it."

But before he could explain further, a strident female voice called out, "You there!"

Wyatt and Cinnabar wheeled toward the nearest house, where an imposing gray-haired woman in gardening togs stood outside her door, scowling at them.

"Us?" said Cinnabar, with her best butter-wouldn't-melt-in-my-mouth expression.

"No, the *other* children trampling my heather!" snapped the woman. "Yes, of course, you. What on earth are you doing in my back garden?"

Wyatt glanced down at Ziggy, who was digging up one of the homeowner's shrubs, then back at the woman. "Walking our dog?" he said.

"Well, walk it somewhere else, or I shall be forced to ring the police!"

With apologies and friendly waves, they dragged the shaggy mutt away. The homeowner's glower tracked them across the next two backyards.

"Holy dooley," said Wyatt. "She's a worse guard dog than an actual guard dog. If we're—"

Harsh barking erupted on the other side of the wall, and a rough voice shouted, "Oi! Where you think you're going?"

Cinnabar and Wyatt instinctively crouched, although the man on the other side couldn't see them. Ziggy whimpered.

"Was that Styx?" Wyatt whispered.

"Shh!" Cinnabar listened intently. A boy's voice answered the man's. Max? They talked back and forth, the man accusing and the boy teasing him. Finally she heard, "You mean she doesn't trust me? I'm wounded."

Definitely Max.

Wyatt's smile was as wide as the Australian Outback, and his blue eyes shone. "That's him!" he hissed.

Cinnabar felt an answering smile spring to her face. The

voices faded as Max and Styx walked away, but her feeling of elation remained.

"Wow," said Wyatt. "He was only ten feet away. Wish we could've sent him a message."

Cinnabar's gaze sharpened, and she gave a curt nod. "Don't you worry," she said, eyes dancing. "We will."

A RIGHT PAIR
OF BERKS

"**BUT WHY** can't we break in right now?" asked Cinnabar, when they'd returned to the van and driven away with their borrowed pet. "They'd never expect it."

"They wouldn't expect it because it's a barmy move," growled Nikki. "Did you take any spy classes at all?"

The two girls glowered at each other, and although Wyatt's sympathies were with Cinn, he knew Nikki had a point.

"We're not ready, that's why," said Mr. Segredo calmly. He piloted the vehicle through thickening traffic as they left the posh neighborhood where LOTUS kept their headquarters.

"So let's *get* ready," said Cinnabar.

Simon Segredo only smiled.

"You've got a plan, haven't you?" said Wyatt.

"Indeed," said Max's father. "We need to stop and pick up a few things."

117

Nikki grimaced. "What, like at a spy shop?"

Mr. Segredo chuckled. "Not exactly. We're going to pay a little visit to some people I know."

An hour later, they'd restored Ziggy to his rightful owner, stopped by a thrift store and a copy shop, and were parked across the street from a row of shabby, unremarkable houses. Mr. Segredo had trained his binoculars on the windows of a unit next to an abandoned store.

"Blast," he muttered. "They're home."

"So," said Tremaine, "are you gonna explain why Wyatt and I are togged out like Boy Scouts, or do we play Twenty Questions?"

Max's father lowered the glasses and nodded at the flat. "That, my young friends, is a LOTUS safe house."

"How do you know?" asked Nikki.

"Duh," said Wyatt. "He used to work with them."

Nikki snarled and tried to reach around Cinnabar to punch him, but the wiry-haired girl blocked her swing.

"Must you always be an utter git?" said Cinnabar.

"Get knotted," snapped Nikki. But she settled back into the seat, arms folded.

"If you're all quite finished," said Simon Segredo stiffly, "I'll continue."

It occurred to Wyatt that Max's father hadn't spent much time around kids, judging by how he reacted to the group's ongoing squabbles. But of course, he'd missed the last seven or so years of Max's life. Being on the run from a worldwide organization of evil spies sure puts a kink in your family time.

Mr. Segredo shifted in the seat so he could face them. "Inside that safe house are all the supplies we'll need for tonight's rescue mission."

"It's tonight?" said Wyatt.

Max's father raised his eyebrows. "The sooner the better, if we're to put a stop to all that adoption rubbish."

"Brilliant." Cinnabar clapped once.

"And these disguises will help how, exactly?" asked Tremaine.

Mr. Segredo eyed their khaki outfits, striped neckerchiefs, and black berets. "All we need is a little distraction."

Nikki snorted. "That's distracting all right. You look like a right pair of berks."

Tremaine ignored her. "So we stroll up to the door in these old-timey uniforms, and then what?"

Mr. Segredo laid out their course of action. After surveying their target for another half hour and spotting no more than two LOTUS agents through the windows, he finally gave them the go-ahead.

Wyatt and Tremaine slipped out of the van on the side away from the safe house. Wyatt began making a beeline for the unit, but Tremaine snagged him by the back of his kerchief.

"Hold up, Horatio," he said.

"What?" said Wyatt.

Tremaine indicated the safe house. "If they see us going straight to their crib and passing up the houses next door, what will they think?"

Wyatt winced. "Too right. Let's start over here." He indicated a nearby house and together they walked up the steps to rap on the yellow door.

"Oo is it?" came a quavery female voice.

"Boy Scouts, mum," said Wyatt. "Can we have a word?"

A long pause, then the clatter of three locks being undone. The door swung open to the length of a security chain, and a pale, wrinkly face, like that of an albino mole, squinted through the crack.

"Yes?" said the old woman.

"We're doing a fund-raiser for our troop, mum," said Wyatt, lifting his clipboard.

"What for?"

Tremaine spoke up. "To raise funds. So that we can go to camp, see?" He waved a sheet of bogus tickets at her.

Her eyes widened at the sight of a tall brown teen on her doorstep.

"A fiver will get you a ticket to our big barn dance," said Tremaine, smiling winningly.

She slammed the door in their faces.

"Friendly sort," said Tremaine.

"Still and all," said Wyatt as they retreated down the walkway, "good thing she didn't buy a ticket."

"Why?" asked Tremaine.

"'Cause then we might actually have to throw a barn dance," said Wyatt. "And I'm allergic to hay."

The tall boy smirked.

Nobody answered the door of the second house they approached. When they reached the sidewalk again, Wyatt did his best not to react to the sight of Mr. Segredo crouching behind a parked car at the curb. He and Tremaine veered up the short walkway to the LOTUS safe house. "Reckon they saw us at their neighbors' place?" Wyatt muttered out of the side of his mouth.

Tremaine shrugged, and the small rucksack on his shoulder swung with the movement. He pressed the buzzer under the house number and unzipped his pack.

The door swung open to reveal a leather-brown man with shoulders like a professional wrestler and a dyed-blond Mohawk.

"Yeah?" he sneered.

"We're raising money for our Scout troop," said Tremaine.

Mr. Mohawk snickered. "Bully for you."

Wyatt offered the LOTUS agent his most winsome, harmless expression. "Help send some poor city kids to camp?"

"Not bloody likely." The agent started closing the door.

Tremaine rummaged in his backpack. "Wait," he said. "Just to show there's no hard feelings, we've got something for you."

Mr. Mohawk's eyebrows rose. "Is it candy?"

"It's pretty sweet," said Wyatt.

Tremaine's hand emerged holding a black-and-yellow Taser pistol. The leads shot out, hitting the LOTUS agent in the chest, and he danced like a spastic disco daddy until he tumbled to the floor.

"See?" said Wyatt. "Sweet."

"It never gets old, mon." Tremaine grinned.

Mr. Segredo dashed up the steps and led the way into the house, weapon drawn. Wyatt and Tremaine were right behind him. They fanned out to right and left, searching for the second agent.

Wyatt felt as useless as mud flaps on a speedboat. The other guys were both armed—Max's dad with a wicked-looking pistol, and Tremaine with the Taser—but what did he have? A ruddy clipboard. Wyatt's shoulders slumped. He was never the lead operative, always the backup. What a joke.

Then Mr. Mohawk groaned and stirred. Wyatt clouted him over the head with the clipboard until it splintered, and the man was silent.

Well, maybe I'm not *completely* useless, thought Wyatt.

Tremaine had climbed noiselessly upstairs to the second story while Mr. Segredo crept through the front room, deeper into the house. Wyatt trailed after Max's dad.

The small house was surprisingly cheery, with framed hunting prints on the walls and a colorful throw on the sofa. The place smelled of fish and chips and furniture polish. A curl of steam rose from a cup of tea on the side table.

Pretty homey for a bad-guy hideout, Wyatt thought.

While he'd paused to check things out, Mr. Segredo had disappeared down a short hall into the kitchen, past a couple of closed doors. Wyatt followed, but just as he drew even with the first door, it swung open to reveal a short Asian man with startled eyes and a chin like a shovel blade.

Wyatt froze.

"Who're you?" the agent demanded.

"I, uh. That is, I . . ." Wyatt stammered.

"Santini!" Shovel Chin called. "Intruder!" And he rushed forward, raising his powerful hands.

Wyatt scrambled backward. Colliding with the side table, he tumbled to the floor amid a shower of table lamp, hot tea, and magazines. "Help!" he squawked, belatedly.

Shovel Chin pounced, and Wyatt rolled at the last second, narrowly missing being pinned.

"Freeze!" shouted Mr. Segredo.

The LOTUS agent twisted like a cat. He grabbed Wyatt's shoulders, hauled him to his feet, and wrapped an arm around his neck, using him as a shield.

"Let him go!" Max's father commanded. He stood in the hallway with arms extended and weapon aimed straight at the enemy spy.

Wyatt heard a metallic *snick* from behind, and felt something cold and sharp prick his neck. He shrank away as far as he could, making a strangled sound.

"How 'bout you drop your pistol instead, and I take you in to Mrs. Frost, you poxy double agent?" Shovel Chin snarled.

Wyatt's mind raced. What to do? Tremaine was still upstairs, and the girls were out in the van. He had no weapon, and the slightest twitch might get his throat slit. Several self-defense moves ran through his head, but if Shovel Chin jerked the wrong way, it was bye-bye, Wyatt.

He froze, too scared to try anything.

"What's it gonna be?" the LOTUS agent said.

Mr. Segredo grimaced. Then he slowly lowered his gun, saying, "Easy. Don't hurt him."

"Set it on the floor and kick it over here. That's right." Shovel Chin gave a nasty chuckle. "And to think that Roscoe Yamada got the best of the great superspy Simon Segredo." He laughed again, and Wyatt got a full dose of onion breath.

Mr. Segredo had placed the gun on the floor, but suddenly he glanced past the LOTUS agent's shoulder.

"Oh, that's rich," said Yamada. "You think I'll fall for *don't-look-behind-you*, the oldest trick in the—"

CRASH! Something shattered close behind Wyatt. The impact drove the LOTUS agent's chin into Wyatt's head like a hammer, while bits of ceramic whatsit showered around them. The man grunted, his grip loosened, and then . . .

KITSSH! A second impact, this one not quite so messy. The agent's body sagged against Wyatt, and both of them collapsed to the floor, Wyatt underneath. Yamada's body blocked Wyatt's field of vision.

"Couldn't let you boys have all the fun," Cinnabar said, from somewhere behind and above.

"Yeah," Nikki seconded. "What kind of sexist rubbish is that, anyway—girls wait in the car while boys take action? Girl spies are just as good as boy spies."

Wyatt agreed with them wholeheartedly. He struggled out from underneath the unconscious agent in time to see an incredible sight: Cinnabar and Nikki exchanging a triumphant fist bump. In their other hands, one held the remains of a table lamp; the other, a heavy vase.

Mr. Segredo knelt and helped Wyatt to stand. "Are you all right?" he asked, concern carved into the lines of his face.

Wyatt nodded. He rubbed his head. "Ow," he said.

Tremaine walked past them, opened the second hallway door, and addressed the others with a grin. "Well, kiss me neck!" he whooped. "Christmas came early."

The rest of the group crowded around the doorway and peered inside. It was like a Spies "R" Us store jammed into a closet—orderly shelves of smoke bombs, weapons, flashbangs, handcuffs, communications devices, disguises, and surveillance equipment, all sitting there waiting for them.

A grin split Wyatt's face. "If this is Christmas," he said, "someone's been a *really* good boy."

CHAPTER 13

NO STEWS IS
GOOD STEWS

IN THE END, Max was surprised at how easy it was to create—a few common household products, some spices from the pantry to disguise the taste, and voilà—a stew fit to give serious intestinal disturbance to a houseful of bad guys. It was so easy, Max thought he just might have to appear on *Celebrity Spy Cook-off* (if he'd actually been a celebrity, and if there had been such a show).

In fact, the hardest part was getting the cook, Mrs. Cheeseworthy, away from her station long enough for him to do the deed.

"Och, lad," she said, brushing back a stray curl with her forearm as she stirred the massive pot of smoked haddock chowder. "Don't hover. I'm trying to work here."

Max leaned against the massive chopping block, watching her. "Sorry, but I've always had an interest in cooking," he lied. "This is fascinating."

He watched the servers come and go with cutlery, napkins, and plates, setting the long table in the formal dining room. The pilfered spice jar dug into his hip, from the pocket where he'd stashed it. Max crossed, then uncrossed his arms. Time was running short—if he didn't spike the stew in the next five minutes, the diners would arrive and it'd be too late.

But Mrs. Cheeseworthy wouldn't budge. She remained as steadfast as a dieter staring down a chocolate cake.

Should he detonate a smoke bomb at the far end of the kitchen? No, too easy to identify, especially for a spy's cook. Set a grease fire? Even worse. Pacing around the food prep island, idly tapping a rhythm on the counter, he even considered pretending to hear someone calling for Mrs. Cheeseworthy. Rubbish idea—she'd never buy it.

So how . . . ?

Purely by accident, his hand brushed the uncorked bottle of wine that had been set out to cool, or breathe, or do whatever wine did. The bottle toppled, falling to the floor with a thud. Pale liquid glugged out onto the floor in a rapidly widening puddle.

"Oh!" said Max, and he didn't have to fake his surprise. "I'm so clumsy."

He cast about the kitchen in a helpless fashion, pretending to search for a dish towel. Snatching up a linen place mat, he made as if to mop up the spill.

"Wait a wee bit," said Mrs. Cheeseworthy, rushing to

rescue it from his hands. "Ye're a bull in a china shop. Let me do it."

Max hid a smile as she went to snag a towel from a rack. Slipping the spice jar into his hand, he stepped over to the stove. "Sorry," he said. "I'll stir this for you."

He waited until she'd squatted down to deal with the mess, then dumped in the spices with one hand and the chemicals with the other. A powdery white residue floated on the surface, but as Max stirred the wooden spoon about, it soon blended in.

He bent over the pot, which was big enough to boil a baby hippo, and took a deep whiff. No strange odors, just fish stew aroma.

"Mmm, smells great," he said.

Mrs. Cheeseworthy dumped the sodden dishcloth in the sink and reclaimed her spoon, elbowing him aside. "Ye've done enough damage for now. Get out of my kitchen. Scat!" As Max headed for the swinging door, she added, "And tell Mr. Leathers to bring out some more Pinot Grigio."

"Right-o," said Max, with a backward wave. "Sorry again."

He had to dodge around the skinny brunette server, who burst through the door exactly as he reached it.

"Beg pardon," she murmured, gaze averted.

As Max pushed through into the dining room, he felt a brief pang to think that Mrs. Cheeseworthy might land in trouble for his little stunt. She seemed like a nice enough woman, for someone who cooked the enemy's chowder. Max shoved that thought aside. He couldn't afford sympathy right now.

The butler, Leathers, was igniting the candlesticks with a wandlike lighter when Max entered.

"The cook says to put out another bottle of Piggo Gigolo," said Max.

The old man's eyebrows slowly climbed his forehead, like a pair of caterpillars on a mountain expedition. "Perhaps she meant Pinot Grigio."

"Perhaps," agreed Max.

Within a handful of minutes, the other diners had arrived. Mrs. Frost glided in with Ebelskeever and Bozzini in tow, all three sharing conspiratorial smiles.

"—traded the brat, so the team should be back soon with the missing piece," the secretary was saying. "All the important ones are in town, and with the device operational, we—" He broke off when he noticed Max at the table. Max wished he could've heard more.

"Ah, young Segredo," said Mrs. Frost. "I trust you had a pleasant morning."

"Absolutely lovely," said Max. "Even took a stroll around the grounds." He was under no illusions—he knew Styx had ratted on him—but the thought of what was about to happen to Frost and company gave him a bubbly feeling inside, like a shaken-up bottle of ginger ale.

Then Vespa sat down across the table, and some of his bubbles went flat. She didn't deserve to suffer through what the rest of the crew was about to experience, but Max couldn't warn her without giving away his plans.

"Hi, Max," she said, with a hopeful smile.

"Vespa," he responded.

The servers bustled into the room carrying a loaf of fresh, crusty bread, a bean casserole, and a bowl of green salad. They served the diners while Mrs. Frost and her assistants turned their conversation to innocuous matters.

Max dug in, as he knew he wouldn't be eating the fish stew. Like scratching a persistent itch in the back of his mind, he wondered again about Hantai Annie, whether she was creeping about the grounds even now. Reluctantly, he tugged his thoughts back on track. Whether she was or wasn't here, he needed to keep to his plan.

Right on cue, the stew arrived, and the servers ladled out generous portions into bowls. Max had to admit, it smelled heavenly.

"Now, that's got a kick to it," said Ebelskeever, after tasting a spoonful. "Old Cheeseworthy's finally spicing up her act."

Mrs. Frost took a ladylike sip and nodded her approval.

Max did his best not to stare as the others tucked into their chowder. In fact, he even pretended to take a few bites himself, making the appropriate yummy sounds. Several minutes passed, and Max was beginning to wonder whether he'd added enough chemicals to have any effect.

His heart shrank. Would he have to come up with a new way to sidetrack the LOTUS crew?

"What's wrong?" asked Vespa. "Don't you like the chowder?"

Max gave a start. "Er, I've never been keen on fish," he said. "It's so . . . fishy."

And just then, someone's stomach made a loud, complaining noise, like the growl of an angry Chihuahua.

Ebelskeever's brow knotted, and his swarthy face turned pale. "Huh," he said.

"What is it, Ronnie?" asked Mrs. Frost, patting her lips with a napkin.

"I feel a bit . . . dodgy."

On the other side of Mrs. Frost, Bozzini mopped his brow. "Too much hot sauce, if you ask me."

Ebelskeever's gut snarled like a wounded wolverine. "I, uh, think I'm . . ." He leaned forward suddenly, clapping his hand over his mouth. *"Hu-unch!* Beg pardon."

Gripping his belly, the big man lurched out of his seat and stumbled away from the table, headed for the nearest bathroom.

"Poor chap," said Bozzini, snickering. "Must have caught a bug or something." Clearly he relished Ebelskeever's discomfort, and he forked some salad into his mouth with relish.

Another stomach complained, quickly answered by a second growl. An expression of distress crossed Vespa's lovely face.

"That's—ooh," she groaned. "I think I caught it too. . . ."

Vespa stood, bent at the waist with thighs clamped together. "I'll just . . ." She nodded toward the doorway and toddled off.

Mrs. Frost's sharp gaze went from Bozzini to Max. "What in the world?"

Belatedly, Max realized he should be showing symptoms too. "Ugh," he groaned, folding forward. "I feel funny."

"How unu—" Mrs. Frost began, until she interrupted herself with a distinctly unladylike belch. An expression of outrage crossed her face, as if her body were an underling who had disobeyed her and would soon face the consequences.

"I . . . later," said Max. He rose and, imitating Vespa, hurried from the room.

Just outside, he peered back through a crack in the door at Bozzini and Frost. LOTUS's chief was sweating profusely. Her face sported the greenish tinge of an unripe avocado. But Bozzini? Her assistant buttered a slice of bread without a care in the world.

Was the man superhuman? Would Max have to find another method to distract him? He kept watching, eye glued to the crack.

"Would you be so kind as to pass the—" Bozzini began.

But he never finished. Instead of words, a brownish liquid exploded from his mouth, spraying across the table with a *blarrrgh!*

Mrs. Frost's lips puckered tighter than a miser's purse strings. Then, through her infuriated expression, she vomited up her lunch with an answering *blarrrgh!*

Only a petty person would take delight in the suffering of others. Max grinned from ear to ear. He hustled away before his dining companions could spot him, keeping up his I'm-so-queasy charade for any cameras that might be watching.

According to Mrs. Cheeseworthy, the rest of the crew ate at the same time as their leaders, except for the guard on the front gate, who took his lunch a half hour later, when his relief arrived. That left Max with something like thirty minutes to duck down into the secret chamber, locate intel on his friends' whereabouts, and make his getaway.

It would be tight, no question.

Max had to make sure the rest of the agents were out of commission. Still nursing his pretend stomachache, he hurried toward the wing where the hired hands ate their meals. He rounded a corner. Down the hall, burly Humphrey was pounding on a door, distress scrawled all over his face.

"Lemme in, mate!" he cried. "Urgent business." But the door didn't open.

As the agent bent double and ralphed into a potted ficus tree, Max smirked and made for the stairs. He shook his head, thinking, I really need to work on my compassion skills. But that was pretty far down on his to-do list.

Charging up the steps two at a time, Max abandoned any pretense at stealth. He had no illusions—they'd tumble to his trick with or without the closed-circuit footage. Right now speed was of the essence.

He strode to Vespa's door and gave it a few quick raps, just to be sure. No answer. Once inside, Max rushed into the bathroom—just like someone who was authentically sick from the stew, if anyone was watching. Here was the real test: Had Vespa told her aunt about his breaking into her office? If so, the connecting door from the shared bathroom would almost certainly boast new, stronger protection.

All was well. After a brief round of lock picking, the door swung open to reveal the murky office interior.

The first thing that hit Max was the odor. It no longer smelled solely of furniture polish and old books, but of buttered popcorn, raw meat, and a deeper, muskier scent. Had the impeccable Mrs. Frost left some food in here to spoil?

Max crept through the dimness toward the desk, but he paused when a strange chuffing sound came from somewhere to his right. The heating duct, perhaps? The noise continued. Max could only make out indistinct shapes in the shadowy room, so he switched on his pocket flashlight and shone it about.

Paintings . . . bookshelves . . . wall . . . And then the

light skittered past a broad patch of white with black stripes surrounding two reflective blue circles. The chuffing sound repeated, and Max's confused brain said, Uh, boss, was that a tiger?

He swung the flashlight beam back, just as a low rumble like a tsunami sucking back from a beach filled the room.

All the tiny hairs on Max's neck and arms stood up.

It *was* a tiger.

And it was staring straight at him.

CHAPTER 14

CROUCHING TIGER, HIDDEN MAX

"AUGH!" An involuntary shout burst from Max at the sight of the massive white tiger crouching by the office door. He scurried backward until his legs bumped against the desk.

The big cat rose and stalked forward on its huge paws, each one bigger than Max's head. Its eerie blue eyes were unwavering.

Max's insides turned to water. His brain roiled with questions, impulses, and utter mind-rending panic. A tiger. A *tiger*?! What the heck was a *big cat* doing roaming around Mrs. Frost's office?

A deeper growl rumbled from the creature's throat.

Max's next thought: And how the heck do I escape without becoming tiger kibble? The predator stood between him and the office door, and it was closer to the bathroom door as well.

Max didn't rate his chances of outrunning a jungle cat, so that left only one way to go: down. He fumbled behind him on the desktop, never taking his eyes off the beast. It had paused, but it was watching him with absolute fascination, like a famished castaway eyeing a Happy Meal.

At last, Max's hand found the lion statuette and pushed on it. As before, a section of the floor slid back, and from the corner of his eye, Max could see the steps leading down to the secret control room. His sanctuary.

He held out a palm toward the predator and edged around the desk.

"Good kitty cat?" he said.

The tiger's muscles bunched, and its tail lashed back and forth. Max vaguely recalled from some nature documentary that this was a sign of aggression.

Uh-oh.

His brain knew that one should never make abrupt movements around predators. But his body had a mind of its own. Max bolted across the few feet separating him from the passageway just as the tiger sprang. Its colossal bulk sailed through the air. Max dove onto the stairs head-first, narrowly avoiding the creature's pounce.

Tucking in his head and arms, Max rolled down the tight cylinder of steps like a whacked-out pinball, blowing past the convenient switch that would've shut the portal behind him. After hitting every step on the way down, he landed with a *whump* on the steel floor.

Although aching and bruised everywhere, Max could tell he'd been lucky. Running his hands quickly across his body, he discovered he hadn't broken anything.

A growl reverberated from the top of the stairs. The hatch!

Lurching to his feet, Max played the flashlight over the wall, hunting for a button that would shut the portal. He spotted a bank of toggle switches on a nearby wall and dove for it, slamming his hand down on all of them.

Lights blazed on, illuminating the equipment lockers, the command center, and its computers. Hearing a sound, Max glanced up the stairwell.

The enormous tiger was padding down the steps, shoulders shifting sinuously with each movement, eyes fixed on Max.

Max fled toward the command center. Where could he hide? The raised platform offered no protection. The cells in the back corridor were locked up tight.

He checked the stairwell. The white tiger was nearly halfway down, and growing more comfortable with negotiating the steps. Max had only a handful of seconds left.

Scrambling around behind the computer bank, he searched for a tall ladder, a loft, anyplace to climb out of reach. Nothing. All that greeted him were metal-and-leather chairs ranged around a glass table.

The tiger snarled, and the sound echoed through the enclosed space like a sky giant's bowling ball barreling down a cloud alley. Max knew how the pin felt.

His gaze lit on the tall metal lockers. There! He grabbed a chair and dashed for the nearest one, jamming the chair up against it. Max stepped up and risked a quick glance at the stairwell.

The tiger had reached the floor. Spotting him, it charged across the room with jaws stretched wide.

Electrified, Max sprang upward, fingertips scrabbling for the top rim of the locker.

He missed.

Once more he leaped, and this time he caught the edge. With a superhuman effort, Max kicked off the chairback, knocking it away, and hauled himself up.

Bam! The beast's body slammed into the metal cabinet, precisely as Max got his legs under him. The whole locker shook, and he had to hang on tightly to avoid being tossed off by the impact.

The big cat chuffed in frustration. It reared onto its hind legs, one paw braced against the locker, the other one swiping at Max, who scooted back out of reach. Despite its seven-foot-long body, the predator could only stretch to the rim of the locker's top with its paw. That was close enough for Max, who eyed the four-inch-long claws whizzing past.

Clearly, the time for stealth had passed. Max imagined that everyone in the mansion had heard the ruckus, so he shouted to scare off the beast.

"Beat it, Stripes!" he cried, waving his arms. "Shove off, you plonker! You're not snacking on me!"

The big cat cocked its head as if to say, *Oh, really?* Then it spread its fanged jaws and hissed like a basketful of cobras. Max could smell its fetid, meaty breath.

Again, it swiped at him, and Max slid back to the other side of the locker. He didn't intend to wait up there like a chump for Humphrey and Dijon to collect him, not if he could help it. Max patted his pockets. No weapons. Nothing but his lock picks, flashlight, and the spices he'd used in the stew.

On impulse, Max uncapped the jar and shook the chili powder over the huge predator. The tiger's eyes widened. It blinked in surprise, and gave a terrific sneeze.

Then it growled again, sneezed once more, and resumed trying to climb onto Max's perch. Its claws raked the metal with a sound like fingernails on a blackboard, but way more menacing. Apparently, tigers didn't like spices.

Keeping a careful watch on the beast's progress, Max reached down into the open side of the locker and fumbled around for a weapon. He wasn't picky. A pistol, a Taser, a speargun—anything would do.

His hand closed around a cool metal tube, and he tugged. Something heavier and bulkier than he'd expected came free, nearly unbalancing him. Max hauled it up and over the rim.

He blinked in surprise. It wasn't a weapon. It looked like an oversize metal rucksack with tubes curling around it and a pair of armrests with joysticks at the end of them.

It was the jet pack.

A grin tugged at Max's mouth, despite his predicament. If a spy had to flee, might as well flee in style.

He slipped the device onto his back and clipped the safety straps across his chest as the big cat slammed the locker once more. Max began examining the dials and buttons, trying to suss out how to operate the thing.

"Oi! What's going on?" a deep voice called. It was Styx, staggering down the last few steps with a whip in his hand.

Oh, great.

"Just enjoying a little quality time with Mr. Whiskers," said Max.

Which was the starter, he wondered, the red button or the black button? And exactly how did you steer this thing?

The agent swayed toward Max and the tiger, one hand clamped over his stomach and a grimace pasted across his features. "Here now," he growled. "Take that gizmo off and— *ooh*—come down here."

Max raised an eyebrow. "Seriously? You did notice that our stripy friend is trying to snack on me?"

Styx groaned, simultaneously clamping his thighs together and folding forward. His face had gone the color of boiled asparagus.

"I got no time for this," he moaned. "Both of you, behave!"

The whip cracked like a car backfiring. At the sound, the tiger slunk away with its ears pinned, grumbling to itself.

Styx braced his hand against a wall of the command center as another wave of nausea rippled through him.

Max experimented with the joysticks and found that they rotated like the ones he'd seen used in action movies. That covered the steering. Probably. But how did you make the jet pack go up and down?

"Styx here," the big man said into a com device. "Intruder in the—*ugh*—control room. Mr. Schnickelfritz on the loose. Request backup. Now."

Max's head snapped up. What kind of name was *Schnickelfritz* for a deadly predator? But more pressing was the realization that if more LOTUS agents were coming, he had to leave now, even without the information he sought.

Here goes nothing, he thought.

Stepping into thin air, he pressed the red button.

Instantly, Max plummeted toward the floor. In desperation, he yanked back on the joysticks as rockets fired behind him with a sound like someone shredding a two-story piece of paper.

Tchoom! Max's stomach dropped into his shoes as he blasted toward the ceiling. He cracked his head on the acoustic tile, punching through the subceiling and into some silver ductwork.

"Stop mucking about!" Styx bellowed. "Don't make me shoot you."

Max pushed the joysticks forward, and his stomach climbed into his throat as the jet pack dove him down at Mr.

Schnickelfritz. The tiger hissed and sprang aside. Barely in time, Max got his feet under him. He slammed onto the floor hard enough to fold him in half like a bendy straw, and then with a flick of the joystick, he was airborne again.

Styx lunged as he passed. Max's trailing foot smacked the spy in the temple as he tore onward.

"Ow!" cried the big man. "Bloody twit."

"Sorry!"

The device took him on a ride as erratic as a pollen-drunk bumblebee's flight pattern. After narrowly avoiding braining himself on a light fixture, Max drove a foot through a computer display and ricocheted into a high-end coffeemaker, spraying hot liquid everywhere. As he tore around the room, frantically levering the joysticks, he discovered that the left one controlled speed and the right one direction. Styx alternately snatched at Max and ducked out of the way, while Mr. Schnickelfritz skulked about by the command center, chuffing at them both.

Wham! Max careened off another locker, whanging his funny bone and making his whole left arm numb. When he tried to shake the arm and bring some life back into it, his sleeve caught on the speed stick. Out of control, Max blasted straight for the stairwell.

Just then, Humphrey and a stiff-faced Dijon came clattering down the steps. At his breakneck approach, their eyes went wide. But to their credit, neither agent fled.

Instead, they braced themselves.

Whomp! Max plowed into the duo at top speed. All three collapsed onto the steps with Max on top.

He struggled to right himself and take off again. But before he could succeed, Humphrey had gripped his arms, pinning him in place. Dijon's hand snaked out and pressed the black button, turning off the jet pack.

"No!" Max cried, thrashing about.

Dijon grunted as his knee connected with her gut. "That's—*oof!*—enough of that." From somewhere, she produced a palm-size Taser, reached up, and gave him a jolt to the neck.

First, a little pinch. Then, every muscle in his body went rigid as the sensation of a million bee stings rushed through him. Max writhed uncontrollably, twitched like a spastic belly dancer, then lay still.

When he opened his eyes again, the first thing Max noticed was a snarling griffin's head in the intricate carved wooden moldings that ran below the ceiling. He groaned.

A grandmotherly face appeared in his field of vision.

"You," said Mrs. Frost, "have caused me a great deal of trouble. And I shan't put up with it any longer."

"Ungh," Max grunted.

"You have damaged my control center, dented my jet pack, given me and my staff intestinal distress, and made my new pet quite peevish."

From somewhere off to his right, the tiger moaned.

"There, there, Mr. Schnickelfritz," said Mrs. Frost.

"Mmfm." Max still couldn't form words properly.

LOTUS's chief leaned closer, until the twin tunnels of her patrician nostrils and her narrowed, smoke-gray eyes filled his view.

"You have lost your freedom of choice," she said, in a voice colder and flatter than an Arctic lake. "Would you like to know what happens now?"

Max nodded.

"You will be locked in your room, *without* your little lock picks. Then, tomorrow we will file some documents, and you will become my ward. Forever."

Max gulped.

Mrs. Frost glared. "And how, as the Americans say, do you like *them* apples?"

"Guh," said Max. But what he meant was, *Not the least little bit.*

CHAPTER 15

THE BIG BOUNCE

AS THE LAST purples of twilight bled into darkness, the sparrows tucked into their eaves to rest. Weary commuters returned home for dinner. And Cinnabar and Wyatt watched Mr. Segredo shoot out security lights with a silenced gun.

"That should do it," he said as the glass from the second lamp tinkled onto the sidewalk.

Now a thirty-foot-long stretch of the wall around LOTUS headquarters was cast into shadow. The three of them crouched behind the shelter of the van, waiting for a response from the LOTUS guardhouse.

Ten minutes passed. None came.

Cinnabar drummed her fingers on the metal paneling.

"Blue Team, we're good to go," Max's father murmured into his com device.

Cinnabar's earbud crackled. "Right then, Red Team,"

came the voice of Mr. Stones, her second-favorite teacher at S.P.I.E.S. "You cupcakes ready to rumble?"

Cinnabar felt a smile spread across her face.

"We were born ready," she said.

"That's an affirmative," said Mr. Segredo drily. "Maintain com silence unless absolutely necessary. Let's go."

Their plan was a simple one, as such plans go. Mr. Stones, along with Tremaine and Nikki, would lop a tree limb so that it fell across the electrified wire that topped the fence. This, hopefully, would short out the wire and draw the attention of the in-house security team; meanwhile, Mr. Segredo, Cinnabar, and Wyatt would hop the fence in a different spot, break into the mansion, and rescue Max.

A simple plan. But simple, as Cinnabar well knew, was not the same as easy.

They gave the Blue Team five minutes to get into position and another ten to chop off the branch. Cinnabar fidgeted, checking and rechecking the time on her cell phone. She had chatted with her sister earlier that day and reassured herself that Jazz was safe. That left only Max.

"Are they going by way of Timbuktu?" she said. "What's keeping them?"

"Patience," said Mr. Segredo.

"It's probably Nikki," said Wyatt. "Bet she's put her foot through someone's window."

"Or face," Cinnabar muttered.

The com device gave three clicks, Mr. Stones's signal that the deed was done.

"Finally," said Cinnabar. "Can we go now?"

"Give it some time," said Mr. Segredo. His face was impassive; Cinnabar figured the man could give polar bears lessons on being cool.

"But—" she began.

He held up a hand. "I know you want to go and save him. So do I. But if we rush in half-cocked, we'll get captured, and how will that help Max?"

Cinnabar sighed. "But I'm about to crawl out of my skin."

"Want to be helpful?" Max's father asked.

"Yes, please."

He passed her a rubber-handled machete. "Take the step-ladder, and go and check the current through the wire with this. Carefully."

"I'll come along," said Wyatt. "Just in case."

Cinnabar rolled her eyes.

They fetched the stepladder from the back of the van. The night air was crisp as an autumn apple. The street smelled of petrol and wood smoke and roast beef from somebody's dinner. All was quiet; residents of the big houses were inside having their meals or away on expensive holidays.

With a wary look in both directions, Cinnabar and Wyatt crossed the road and leaned the stepladder up against LOTUS's brick perimeter wall.

"Simon says, gloves," whispered Wyatt.

"Gloves?" she replied.

He dug his own pair from a jacket pocket. "As in, Simon says, wear your gloves for extra safety."

She sighed again but went along with his request. As Wyatt braced the stepladder, Cinnabar climbed to the second-highest step and reached down for the machete. Wyatt passed it up, handle first.

"Now be extra careful not to touch—" he said.

"The metal part of the blade," she interrupted. "I'm not a complete berk, you know. I do have a few brain cells to rub together."

He raised a palm. "Didn't want anything to happen to you," he said.

"Don't get mushy."

Wyatt smirked. "Who's mushy? It's only that the smell of fried Cinnabar would be hard to get out of my nostrils."

She snorted at his comment, but she did make doubly sure that no part of her hand was touching the metal blade. Then, Cinnabar stretched her arm up to its fullest extent, and with an involuntary grimace, gingerly touched the machete to the razor wire.

No sparks, no jolt. Nothing.

Both of them let out their breath. "Cowabunga!" Wyatt crowed.

Cinnabar shushed him.

"Beauty," he whispered. "Our plan is *working.*"

"So far," said Cinnabar, passing back the machete.

Wyatt gave a thumbs-up to Mr. Segredo and hurried over to the van. He returned with two rubber floor mats, which he handed up to Cinnabar, who draped them side by side over the razor wire.

Mr. Segredo slipped from the vehicle like a shadow and motioned for Wyatt to join him. Together, they carted over a professional-quality mini-trampoline and set it up beside the wall.

"Remember," he said, "if either of you isn't comfortable with this, you can always—"

A dog's yap interrupted him.

The trio whirled to see an old man, as bent as a question mark, following a scrappy little Scotty dog up the sidewalk. Mr. Segredo leaned against the ladder, trying to camouflage it. Nothing could be done about the trampoline.

The old man shuffled up and fixed it with a bleary eye. "What's all this, then?"

"Trampoline," said Wyatt with a guileless grin.

"Mini-tramp, actually," Cinnabar corrected.

Mr. Segredo spread an arm expansively. "Merely making sure the kids get some exercise," he said. "Tearing 'em away from the computer, you know how it is."

"Nope." The man's dog sniffed the trampoline while its owner squinted at the ladder. "And what's that for?"

"Gives 'em more height, you see," said Simon Segredo. "For a bigger bounce."

The dog walker grunted, tugged the dog's leash, and began to shuffle on past. Cinnabar slumped in relief, but then the man turned back to them.

"You live in that whopping great house behind the wall?" he asked.

"Yes," said Cinnabar and Mr. Segredo at the same time as Wyatt answered, "No."

She glared at the blond boy. "He's visiting. Why do you ask?"

"Tch," the old man tutted, shaking his head. "Such odd noises coming from there, day and night. Like a regular zoo, it is."

Mr. Segredo raised a calming hand. "Sorry about that. We'll try to keep it down."

With a final harrumph, the man led his dog out of sight.

"What do you reckon all that was about?" Wyatt asked.

"No idea," said Max's father. "Time to go." He moved the ladder to the proper spot, in line with the mini-tramp and the mat-draped section of the wire.

Cinnabar volunteered to go first. She scaled the step-ladder to the top, pumped her arms, and leaped onto the rebounding surface.

Once, twice, three times she bounced, higher and higher. Then Cinnabar gave the hardest jump of all, tucked her limbs, and shot up . . . and over the wall!

Some low shrubs broke her fall on the other side. Not a

perfect landing perhaps—the Russian judges wouldn't give it a ten—but good enough for espionage work.

"Well?" Mr. Segredo's whisper cut through the darkness.

"Made it," she whispered back, a fierce exhilaration filling her. "Next?"

Wading through the bushes until she was out of the way, Cinnabar made a quick scan of her surroundings. A narrow rim of shrubs grew just inside the wall, giving way to a wide swath of lawn. Beyond that, dimly illuminated by tasteful spotlights, lay a tennis court, and beyond that the hulking sprawl of the mansion, its lights blazing through the darkness.

She listened intently. No guards came running, no dogs barked.

So far, so good.

Cinnabar heard grunted exhalations from the other side of the wall. Then, like a blond-haired moon, a round face rose into view, followed by a flailing body. But Wyatt's efforts, rather than carrying him farther, landed him in trouble. As he descended, one outflung arm caught on the uncovered razor wire.

Shhhrick! His jacket sleeve tore, yanking him off course. Wyatt thumped against the brick wall and tumbled clumsily into the bushes.

"All right?" she whispered.

He crunched through the shrubbery to her side, plucking at his bottom. "This spandex is riding up my bum, but otherwise, yeah—I'm aces."

About thirty seconds later, the lanky form of Simon Segredo flew over the wall, looking like nothing so much as a too-tall Olympic gymnast. He executed a flip and even stuck the landing.

"Stone the crows," Wyatt muttered, eyes wide.

"Show-off," whispered Cinnabar.

Sizing up the situation in a glance, Max's father led them along the edge of the lawn at a slow jog, approaching the mansion obliquely. Two-thirds of the way there, he paused in the cover of an overhanging tree.

Cinnabar tapped his shoulder and indicated the rambling structure ahead. "A dumb question," she said. "How do you know which of those sixty-something rooms we'll find Max in?"

Mr. Segredo's teeth gleamed in the faint moonlight. "GPS," he said.

"No way," said Wyatt. "You had a tracker on Max and they didn't catch it?"

"Not for two whole days," said the spy. "Last I saw, he was staying in a third-floor room, in the nearest wing of the house."

Wyatt beamed. "Same way I found him last time Max got himself into LOTUS HQ." He turned to Cinnabar. "Remember, Cinn?"

She patted his shoulder. "Memory lane later. Rescue now."

"Too right."

Mr. Segredo unzipped a small gear bag and passed each

of them a metal canister. "You know your targets. Hurry now, and don't get spotted."

"Good-o," said Wyatt. "Where do we meet?"

Max's father pointed. "That corner, soon as you can. Now go!"

The three of them split up, one for each wing of the grand estate. Cinnabar marveled anew at how easily Wyatt had hacked the mansion's floor plan and heating-system schematics. She shook her head admiringly. That boy had mad computer skills. Too bad he turned into a drooling idiot around pretty girls.

Each wing possessed its own heat pump, and each heat pump, Wyatt discovered, had an air intake vent that was accessible from outside the house. Cinnabar located her target behind a low hedge. Squatting beside it, she fished the smoke grenade from her jacket pocket. With a quick jerk, she pulled the ignition ring and lobbed the cylinder into the vent.

Billows of bluish smoke trailed behind it as the bomb disappeared. Cinnabar grinned. Hot times in LOTUS HQ.

She made for their rendezvous, sticking to the shadows in case any of the residents happened to glance outside. As she passed a room that was lit up like a diorama, a scowling, apelike man loomed at the window, a sudden apparition.

Ebelskeever!

Cinnabar tucked into a crouch and held her breath. Had he spotted her?

Her heart thudded and it felt like ants were crawling on the inside of her skin. Seconds ticked past. She didn't dare move, but she had to know. As slowly as a winter thaw, she uncurled enough to raise her eyes to the window. The burly man stood there still, dark eyes peering unseeing into the night, and mouth working as he spoke with someone in the room.

Then, a muffled yell. Ebelskeever's face registered alarm, and he spun away, disappearing from view. The smoke must've begun to emerge from the heating vents.

Staying low, Cinnabar dashed to the meeting spot. Wyatt was already waiting, shifting from foot to foot, and Mr. Segredo arrived right after her.

"Let's move," he said. "We've got ten to fifteen minutes, tops. If we hit trouble, Blue Team won't be coming to the rescue—they're only for distraction."

"So let's not get in trouble," said Cinnabar.

Mr. Segredo sent them each a searching look, then stuck out his hand, palm down. "For Max," he said.

Cinnabar and Wyatt stacked their hands on top of his. "For Max," they echoed.

When a wide-eyed LOTUS agent burst through the nearby side door, they quickly stunned him, hid the unconscious man in the bushes, and slipped inside the mansion.

CHAPTER 16

NIGHTS IN BLACK SPANDEX

ALARMS WAILED like heartbroken robots. Billows of blue-gray curled from heating vents. Voices shouted back and forth, and the acrid smell of smoke stained the air.

Wyatt's heart throbbed like that techno music Cinnabar's sister fancied, but he didn't much feel like dancing. He hustled down the hall behind the others, gripping a pistol in his sweaty palm. It didn't matter that the gun was loaded with beanbag rounds; what worried him was the mission.

Truth is, he was rubbish at this operational stuff. Give him a computer, a gizmo, or an electrical system and he was a regular legend—none better. But all this creeping about, shooting, and karate-kick stuff made him feel like the last kid chosen for the football team—clumsy, out of place, and ill prepared.

He hoped he wouldn't let Max down.

Mr. Segredo led them along the brightly lit hall, Taser in one hand, pistol in the other. They hurried past empty illuminated rooms that appeared to be a stage set for a play called *Rich People's Lives Are Better than Yours* (minus the smoke, of course). Wyatt had never seen such posh decor, such luxurious furniture—except maybe at the *other* LOTUS HQ he'd invaded. Say what you might about the enemy, they could do a mean decorating job.

Two women dressed in black-and-silver spandex uniforms hurried down the hall from the other direction. Wyatt tensed, then he realized why Max's father had insisted they wear the togs they'd discovered in the LOTUS safe house.

"Where's the fire?" asked the lead agent, a blond woman with the broad shoulders of a professional swimmer.

"We can't find it," said Mr. Segredo, taking a couple of steps aside. "Have you tried the boiler room?"

The darker woman's gaze took in his weapons and the two teens accompanying him. She frowned. "Since when do we hire kids?"

"It's a recent thing," said Wyatt. "New internship program."

Still confused, the women looked between the tall agent and his charges. Blond Swimmer's hand unconsciously moved toward the holster strapped under her arm.

Cinnabar poured on the charm. "I can't believe how lucky I am to be an intern," she gushed. "All I want is to be a top agent, like you two."

Their attention focused on Cinn. To one side, Wyatt noticed Mr. Segredo readying his weapons. His stomach knotted; he really didn't want to see bloodshed.

"Me too," Wyatt added, forcing a hero-worshiping grin. "Stuff a duck and strike me bloody handsome! I'm happier than a tick on a fat dog!"

"Is English his second language?" the darker agent asked Cinnabar.

"We're not sure what his first one is," she replied.

Blond Swimmer rolled her eyes and waved them forward. "Get on with you. This is an emergency, not a guided tour."

"Come along, kids," said Mr. Segredo.

"Ta, then." Wyatt ducked his head in thanks.

"And keep an eye out for the fire source," the other woman called after them as the S.P.I.E.S. team continued on their way.

Soon they reached an intersection where their smaller corridor met the main one, and Mr. Segredo's steps slowed.

"We go right," said Wyatt, consulting his smartphone. "According to the floor plan, the stairs are that way."

With a curt nod, the tall spy strode down the right-hand hall. They had nearly reached the staircase when a bulky, muscular figure emerged from a side room.

"Ebelskeever," said Max's father.

"Segredo," said the LOTUS agent. His shoulders flexed.

For a millisecond, they froze, wolfish grins on their faces.

As Mr. Segredo raised his pistol, Ebelskeever moved with startling swiftness. He struck the Beretta from the tall spy's grip and seized the hand that held the Taser, slamming it against the wall. The weapon fell to the carpet.

The two agents grappled, swaying. In a judo throw, Mr. Segredo tossed the bigger man over his hip, but before he could recover his weapons, Ebelskeever landed lightly and aimed a sweep kick at him. Max's father dodged. When the LOTUS agent reached for the Taser, Mr. Segredo blasted a roundhouse kick at his head, driving him back.

Although Ebelskeever was larger and heavier, they seemed evenly matched in skill. The men raged up and down the corridor, punching and kicking. Snatching up the Taser, Wyatt tried to pass it to Mr. Segredo, but Max's father couldn't look away from the other man for even a split second. Cinnabar balanced on the balls of her feet, seeking an opening to join the attack on the enemy spy.

"Find the asset," Mr. Segredo snapped. "Go!"

Wyatt hesitated, then jammed the Taser into his belt and yanked on Cinn's sleeve. Reluctantly, she came away, and both of them dashed for the stairs. Up and up they pounded, footfalls whispering like secrets on the plush ivory carpet.

At the third floor, Cinnabar took the lead. Closed doors lined the wide, quiet corridor.

"Which one?" she asked.

"Fourth door . . . on the left . . . I think," Wyatt panted.

Cinnabar tried the knob. The door swung open to reveal a small sitting room, as empty as a gambler's bank account.

"Wyatt . . ."

"Or was it . . . third door . . . on the right?" he wondered aloud, planting his hands on his knees and wheezing. He really had to start exercising more often. Or at all.

Cinnabar threw up her hands. "You mean you don't know where he is?"

Wyatt shrugged. "A GPS isn't . . . all that accurate."

"And you waited until *now* to mention it?"

Hands still resting on his knees, Wyatt swung his head, examining the nearby doors. Among those he could see, only one of them boasted a newly installed dead bolt on the outside.

"There." He pointed.

With a soft cry, Cinnabar rushed to the door. By the time Wyatt joined her, she'd already broken out her picks and was working on the dead bolt.

"Hurry," said Wyatt helpfully. He glanced down the corridor. They were still alone. So far.

"You want this to go faster?" Cinnabar said around the pick between her teeth. "Tackle that second lock."

"On it," said Wyatt. He broke out his own set of tools and began tinkering with the doorknob.

"Who's there?" came a faint voice from the other side of the door.

Cinnabar pressed her cheek to the wood. "Max, it's me—Cinnabar."

"And Wyatt," Wyatt added. "Come to spring you, mate."

"Brilliant!" Max sounded relieved. "Get me out of here!"

"Happy to," said Cinnabar, "if you'll stop distracting us."

"Oh, right," said Max. "Sorry." After a pause, he added, "Do hurry, though."

Wyatt and Cinnabar focused on their work, and in another few minutes, the locks clicked open. Turning the knob, Cinnabar hurried into Max's arms for a fierce hug. This went on for several heartbeats longer than was comfortable for Wyatt to watch, so he shuffled his feet and studied the carpet.

"You came for me," Max said at last, stepping free of the embrace and looking from one friend to the other. His eyes shone, and he gripped Wyatt around the top of the shoulders in a manly clinch.

"Well, yeah," said Wyatt. "Didn't want you to have all the fun."

"But how—?"

"Let's go." Placing a hand on each of their backs, Cinnabar propelled them into the hall. "It's a long story. And in case you hadn't noticed, we're in the bad guys' house."

They jogged for the staircase. "But how did you get in?" asked Max. "And why are you dressed like that?"

"We met your dad, we raided a safe house, he made a plan,

we broke in," said Wyatt as the trio scrambled downstairs.

"Huh," Cinnabar mused. "I guess it's not *that* long of a story."

They hit the second-floor landing and pressed on, ever downward, the thick carpet swallowing their footsteps.

"Wait, my father's here?" said Max.

"Too right he is," said Wyatt. "We left him fighting Ebelskeever, and—"

Max seized Wyatt's arm, yanking him to a stop. "Where?"

"First floor," said Wyatt.

"And he's fighting *Ebelskeever*?" Max raked a hand through his hair. "Do we have any weapons?"

Wyatt struggled to tug the Taser out of his belt. "There's this, for starters." Max accepted the weapon and pushed ahead.

Cinnabar caught at Max's shoulder. "He told us to get you out," she said. "We should go."

An unreadable expression crossed his face. "Not without my dad."

Wyatt noticed that it was the first time Max had referred to his father as "dad." He wondered if it meant anything.

"Your father wants you out of here," said Cinnabar.

"And what, I just leave him behind? I didn't notice you abandoning your sister when things got tough."

Cinnabar sized up their friend, her lips clamped tightly. She nodded once. "Okay. We'll take a quick peek around."

When the little group reached the ground floor, Cinnabar and Wyatt headed left, toward where they'd left the combatants.

The hallway was deserted.

"Not good," said Wyatt.

In fact, now that he noticed it, the whole place was quiet. Too quiet. No more wailing smoke alarms, no more shouting agents.

"Where is he?" Max asked.

"Dunno." Cinnabar reversed direction and headed back toward where they'd entered the mansion. "Come on, we don't have time to look."

"Wait," Wyatt said. "We should take a different way out."

Cinnabar put her hands on her hips. "Don't be daft."

"No, listen to me," said Wyatt, surprised at how forceful he was being. "By now, they know we caused the smoke, and they know where we broke in. They'll be expecting us to use the same route. Won't they?"

He could read his friends' faces, almost as if he were reading their thoughts. *Wyatt's the tech guy—what does he know about operations?*

Max shook his head. "Wyatt, I have to find my dad."

"Too late," said Cinnabar, planting her feet in a wide stance. "We need to take the escape route we know."

Wyatt's jaw clenched. Ten minutes into their rescue, and already things were falling apart.

Sudden heat rose from his gut, as if he'd just chugged a lava milk shake and it didn't want to stay down. These were supposed to be his friends. Why wouldn't they listen to him? Why did they always treat him like a total dill?

"Fine!" he roared. "Find your own way out." And he whirled and stomped off down the hallway, the image of their stunned faces seared into his mind.

Wyatt's skin buzzed. His brain churned. He couldn't believe he'd done that; he also couldn't believe he'd waited so long to do it. It felt liberating; it felt awful. Finally, after a minute, he could resist no longer. He glanced back for his friends.

They hadn't followed.

Doubt washed over him. Had he been too harsh? Or worse, had his idea been a bad one?

Around the corner, footsteps scuffed against the carpet. Rough voices echoed. Slipping into the nearest room, Wyatt closed the door nearly all the way, and peered through the crack.

Two hard-faced men in midnight-blue suits raced past. Their voices reached him like words blown from a speeding car.

"—trying to steal the device?" one was asking.

"They couldn't," the other replied. "It just got here. Still, we have to . . ."

After they'd gone, Wyatt peeked outside. If those two

agents were chasing Max and Cinnabar, he had to do something. He couldn't let LOTUS take his friends, no matter how pigheaded they were acting.

Wyatt crept along the hallway after the two spies, hugging the wall and prepared to duck into hiding at any time. When he reached the intersection they'd passed on their way into the mansion, he sank to the carpet and peered around the corner.

Good thing he did, too.

Because what Wyatt saw left him as dazed as a stunned mullet.

CHAPTER 17

HARD CELL

IF MAX SEGREDO had been asked to list the least favorite moments of his life so far, this particular moment would definitely rank among the top five.

His father, Simon Segredo, stood battered and bleeding in handcuffs, surrounded by LOTUS agents. More of these very same agents leveled large, no-nonsense guns at Max and Cinnabar. And off to one side, beaming like she'd just been handed the keys to the city and a brand-new Rolls-Royce, stood none other than Mrs. Frost.

"Well, well," she cooed. "Such a touching scene. Father and son, back together again."

Eyes as steely as a boxful of knives, Simon Segredo met her gaze. "Let him go," he said.

Ebelskeever sniggered, a sound like a grizzly bear choking on a ham bone. "Seems to me, you're in no position to make demands, *mate*," he said, giving the last word a sarcastic twist. Max was pleased to note the big goon's bruised face and right eye swelling shut. His father had clearly given Ebelskeever as good as he'd gotten.

Simon ignored the man. "Max served his purpose," he told Mrs. Frost. "He brought me here. Now let them go."

The LOTUS chief tugged on her sleeves with an amused smile. "Just when things are getting interesting? I think not."

An ache clutched Max's heart at the beaten expression his father tried to hide. No matter what Simon might have done in the past, no matter how mixed up Max's feelings about him, the man's pain was impossible to ignore.

"I won't fight it," Max blurted.

"How's that?" Mrs. Frost's eyebrows lifted.

Max felt like he'd swallowed lead weights. "The adoption." He couldn't look at her. "I'll agree to it, if you let them go."

Cinnabar gasped. Simon's fists clenched, his stare was wounded.

Chuckles percolated from Ebelskeever and the other agents. "Ooh, how noble," the big man crooned. "A bloody pair of martyrs, the both of you." His gaze swung to Cinnabar. "How 'bout you, girlie? Where's your noble gesture?"

"How's this?" she said, making a rude hand motion. "Get stuffed."

The LOTUS agents roared with laughter, which cut off like a light switch at Mrs. Frost's glare.

"Really," she huffed. "There's simply no excuse for vulgarity." The corridor full of evil spies looked like a pack of school pranksters being chastised by a headmaster.

Order restored, the LOTUS chief regarded Max. "We won't be taking you up on your generous offer—"

"But—" Max began.

"It's clear you'll never come around to our way of thinking—although I may have another way for you to be of use. And now . . ." Her attention shifted to Simon Segredo. "You know what I want. Let's have it."

He shook his head. "Release them first."

"You don't listen very well, do you?" She rubbed her hands together briskly. "A common problem with people of your generation. But perhaps a round or two of torture will help focus your mind."

"I can take whatever you dish out," said Simon.

Mrs. Frost's cheeks dimpled. "Who said we'd be torturing *you*?"

Max gulped but tried to hide his fear. His father hadn't even flinched.

"Ronnie, would you please?" said the spymaster.

At a shooing motion from Ebelskeever's pistol, two dark-suited agents gripped Simon's biceps and frog-marched him down the hall. A broad-shouldered blond woman gave Max a shove to encourage him to follow.

As he and Cinnabar fell in behind his father, Max caught her eye and mouthed, "Wyatt?"

But Cinnabar only lifted her eyebrows and shrugged.

. O. O. O.

The chill of their subterranean cell penetrated all the way to Max's bones in the first ten minutes. But that discomfort was nothing compared to his conversation with his father.

They sat on facing cots in the cramped, harshly lit room while Cinnabar paced, inspecting their prison.

"I can't believe you offered to let that witch adopt you," she said. "Have you gone over to the dark side, or are you completely mental?"

Max just shook his head.

"That was brave," said Simon, "offering to trade yourself for us."

"Yeah, I guess," said Max. "You did the same thing."

Max was having a hard time focusing on his father's words. Conflicting feelings bound up his mind and heart like battling pythons. On the one hand, Simon had put himself in danger to come rescue him—that counted for a lot. But on the other hand, he'd worked with LOTUS before and didn't exactly have a sterling record of loyalty and reliability. Was he truly on their side this time?

Plus, some older, deeper issues bubbled beneath the surface. . . .

"Son, it wouldn't have made any difference," said Simon. "No matter what you offer, Frost will never let me go. I've got something she needs."

"Charm?" said Max. "A warm-blooded body?"

"Information." Max's father leaned forward, bracing his elbows on his knees. The stark overhead light turned his eyes and cheeks into pockets of shadow. "When I worked with them, I stole evidence of various crimes they committed, as insurance. Should something . . . unfortunate happen to me, it would be released. And when that evidence finds its way into certain hands . . ."

"I get it," said Max. "Bye-bye, LOTUS."

"Precisely."

A sour taste filled Max's mouth as he remembered the compliments Mrs. Frost had paid him. *You're the best natural spy I've seen.* "So all of her flattery, the whole adoption thing, that was only a ruse to flush you out?"

"That's how she operates."

"What a sweetheart," said Cinnabar, glancing over from her inspection of the door.

"Tell me the truth," Max asked his father. "If you hadn't heard she was trying to adopt me, would you still have come after me?"

"Of course." A bolt of pain flashed through his father's eyes. "To the ends of the earth, Max. I hope you know that."

"Really?" Max's head throbbed and his jaw felt tight. Suddenly he couldn't bear to sit still, so he jackknifed to his feet. "And *how* would I know that?"

"Max, I—"

"You've been gone over half of my life. When you finally show up, you trick me into betraying my friends and try to get me to join LOTUS. And you think that makes you Father of the Year?"

Cinnabar's lips pursed in an O. As the words were leaving his mouth, a part of Max was horrified by what he was saying. He didn't want to talk about all this in front of Cinnabar. But he couldn't stop.

"If I know anything, it's that you can't be trusted," he continued, waving his hands. "Every time you're up against it, you chose yourself first—not me."

Simon looked like he'd been gut-punched. But his voice came out low and steady. "Every time but this time."

He was right. Max hated that he was right, but his father really had risked everything to save him tonight. His fists clenched, then relaxed.

"Max, I've not been the world's best father—"

"Understatement of the year," Max muttered, sitting back down and turning toward the wall.

"—but I want to be," said Simon. "If you'll give me another chance."

For a score of heartbeats, Max rested his forehead against the cool metal surface, sorting through his feelings. At last he said, "You want to be a good father? Start by telling me the truth."

Simon Segredo's glance went from Cinnabar, to the security camera above them, then back to Max. He took a deep breath and spread his hands. "I'm an open book. Ask me anything."

Did he really mean it? Max spun back to face him, mouth as dry as ashes. The question he'd never gotten answered found its way to his lips. "My mum . . . How—how did she die?"

Openmouthed, Cinnabar looked from one of them to the other, her search of the cell forgotten.

Max's father blew out a sigh. He rubbed his face and stared at the floor. "Max, I wanted to spare you that."

"I'm not a kid anymore," said Max with some heat. He waved a hand at their prison. "If I'm old enough to be locked up by enemy spies, I'm old enough to know the truth."

Simon regarded him with a new light in his eyes. "You're right. You're not the little boy I left behind. Sometimes I forget."

"So?"

Max's father shook his head and winced. He sighed again, heavily.

"Mrs. Frost . . ." Max cleared his throat. "She says you were responsible for Mum's death."

"In a way, she's right."

Max stiffened. "What?"

Cinnabar stepped to his side, laying a hand on his shoulder.

Max's insides felt like a shaken-up Coke can, ready to explode at the slightest provocation. He couldn't seem to catch his breath.

"Your mother was a spy," said Simon, his voice flat. "Like us."

"No way!" burst from Cinnabar's lips.

Max sat frozen in place. "But . . ."

A sad smile played across Simon's face. "That's how we met. She quit active duty just before you were born, but she was a top agent."

So many questions raced through Max's mind. Who did she spy for? How did they meet? But one question overrode them all. "If she quit, then how . . . ?" he asked.

Simon glanced up at Max, then down at his palms. "I, er . . ." He coughed. "I took an important assignment that drew the attention of LOTUS. They tried to stop me from completing my mission, by any means necessary."

"They—they killed her to stop you?" Max's throat muscles clenched so tightly he could barely get the words out.

His father grimaced, staring at the wall beside Max as if watching a movie play on it. "She was out of the game, safe at home. Our boss thought I was too hot, so he asked her to make a simple pickup from a dead drop. He thought she'd be off their radar, you see?"

"And . . . ?" Cinnabar prompted, caught up in the story.

Simon's gaze flicked over to her, but the past had him in its grip. A single tear welled up in his eye. "She was so beautiful, your mother. And selfless—" He choked up, and the tear rolled down his cheek. "I begged her not to go, but she wanted to protect me. She wanted you to grow up knowing your father."

The knot in Max's throat now felt like a fist. He was rooted in place, only dimly aware of Cinnabar's hand on his shoulder.

"How, er, did it . . . ?" he managed to say.

"It was raining," said his father. "She kissed me, and she went to make the pickup. I couldn't bear the thought of her out there alone, so I left you with a friend and followed. I arrived too late."

The sides of Max's mouth tugged down. He almost forgot to breathe.

Fresh tears leaked from Simon's eyes, and he made no effort to wipe them away. "By the time I reached the rendezvous, she . . ." He gulped. "She was gone. Floating in the river."

"LOTUS?" said Max.

"LOTUS."

A sudden rage swept through Max like a forest fire. His pulse pounded in his ears and his fists clenched, but he found himself curiously still, his senses heightened.

Outside their cell, a machine hummed faintly. Somewhere in the mansion, water gurgled through pipes. The moment felt fragile, like the tiny robin's egg Max had found in one of his fosters' backyards, ages ago.

"I—" he began, but the snick of a card reader and the scrape of keys in the lock cut him off.

The door swung open. Ebelskeever and Humphrey stepped inside, guns drawn. Two other agents flanked the door. The burly spy motioned Max, Cinnabar, and Simon toward the back wall with a wave of his pistol.

And in stepped Mrs. Frost, wearing a mock-solicitous expression. "Awfully sorry to intrude on family time."

Max's jaws clamped together so tightly he thought his molars would grind to dust. More than anything, he wanted to wipe that expression off her face. He glanced at Simon, expecting the same reaction.

In a blink, his father transformed from grieving widower into impassive secret agent. The bland mask was back in place.

"Make yourself at home," said Simon, gesturing to the crowded cell. "*Mi casa, su casa.*"

Mrs. Frost stood inside the doorway, head slightly cocked, an agreeable smile on her face.

With a supreme effort, Max hid his rage behind an ice-cold wall. "Can we get you something?" he said, taking the cue from his father. "Stale bread and water? Cobwebs?" His mind was still reeling from the revelations about his mother.

"Actually, I have something for you," said Mrs. Frost, snapping her fingers. "Remember I was saying we'd find a way for you to prove your usefulness?"

"Yeah?" said Max guardedly.

Vespa stepped into the doorway, wearing an expression that said *Sorry about this.* In her hands she carried a familiar blue cube and high-tech headset.

The mind-control device.

"Here it is," said Mrs. Frost. "And all you have to do is test-drive our newest toy."

Max flinched. "You want to brainwash me?"

"*Au contraire,*" said the grandmotherly spymaster. "That's not my intention at all."

He relaxed a little.

"I want you to brainwash Cinnabar."

CHAPTER 18

A STICKY SITUATION

MAX WAS utterly gobsmacked. He stared at the placid, white-haired woman as if she'd suddenly sprouted horns and started singing pop tunes in Urdu.

"Brainwash . . . ?"

"Your young lady friend there," said Mrs. Frost. "I would ask you to try it on your father, but we haven't yet calibrated the machine. And I would be truly vexed if certain information was accidentally erased from his mind. That would be tragic."

"Tragic," said Max woodenly.

She raised her eyebrows. "So you'll comply?"

"You can't force him to," snapped Simon Segredo.

"Certainly not," said Mrs. Frost, as if addressing a simpleton. "That's why I'm giving him a choice—one that will affect his future. So, Max? What do you say?"

Vespa bit her lip.

Cinnabar hugged herself. Her eyes were wide and wary.

"For you?" said Max to the spymaster. "Absolutely not."

Mrs. Frost folded her arms. "This is a onetime offer," she said. "Refuse it, and you'll meet the same fate as your fellow prisoners."

"I wouldn't have it any other way." Max felt a sudden lightness at the abandonment of his double-agent status. "They're family, and family members should all be treated equally. But I guess you wouldn't know about that"—he cut his eyes toward Vespa—"would you?"

Vespa glanced away. Mrs. Frost bared her teeth in a caricature of a smile.

"Stooping to personal attacks is a mark of low breeding," she said in a pitiless tone. Her eyes were gray marbles.

Max barked a laugh. "And beating up my father and forcing me to brainwash my friend is how the posh people do it? Then I'm a peasant every time."

The only sign of Frost's displeasure was a slight flaring of the nostrils. "You are unforgivably rude and should be punished. But I would never strike a child." She glanced at Ebelskeever. "Strike this child."

Whap! The big man's open-handed slap snapped Max's head around and sent him tumbling onto the cot. His cheek felt like it was aflame.

With a growl, Simon lunged at the agent. Humphrey

stepped in the way, jamming his pistol up under Simon's chin.

"Ah-ah-ah," said Mrs. Frost. "Temper, temper."

Simon's glare could've melted diamonds, but his voice stayed smooth. "You haven't even seen me lose my temper yet."

The whole side of Max's face throbbed with a dull ache. He couldn't believe Ebelskeever had struck him. The gloves were truly off now—on both sides. He began contemplating how he would avenge his mother and burn LOTUS to the ground.

Mrs. Frost tossed Max a dismissive glower. "I'm done with you, boy. You're still willful and misguided, despite all my best efforts."

Max sent up a silent thank-you for his natural rebelliousness.

"But you . . ." Mrs. Frost's gaze lasered in on Simon. "I've got a proposal for you."

"Can't wait," said Cinnabar.

Frost ignored her. "Give me what you took, and I'll let Max go free."

Simon glanced from his son to the white-haired woman. "And what guarantee do I have?"

"My honor as a lady," said Mrs. Frost stiffly.

Max's father arched an eyebrow. "Knowing that you have personally been responsible for hundreds, maybe thousands of deaths, and countless crimes? You'll have to forgive me if I can't quite trust that guarantee."

Clenching her jaw, Mrs. Frost snapped, "This is becoming tiresome. We shall have to calibrate this invention, and then we shall return. At that point, you will give me what I desire, or I shall begin brainwashing the entire lot of you—starting with *you*." She scowled at Max, and he somehow managed not to spontaneously combust at her wrath.

With that, LOTUS's chief spun on her heel and strode from the room, chin held high. Sending Max a worried glance, Vespa trailed after her aunt.

"Pity about the brainwashing," sneered Ebelskeever. "I hear tell it sometimes goes squiffy, leaving the subject a total cabbage. Though with you three, the hardest part will be telling before from after."

The other agents snickered as if this was the height of wit, and they swaggered out, relocking the cell securely.

"Charming bunch," said Max. He tried for a carefree expression, but a chill like snowmelt trickled down his spine.

"And what a delightful proposition," said Simon. "Any thoughts?"

"Just one," said Max. "Let's be long gone when they get back."

"Agreed," said Simon and Cinnabar together.

"And how exactly do we accomplish that?" Cinnabar asked.

Max scanned the cell. "There's got to be a way out of here."

Simon shared a conspiratorial look, glanced at the security camera in the upper corner, and lowered his voice to a near whisper. "Every prison has its weaknesses. It's merely a matter of finding them. Cinnabar, what did you notice during your inspection?"

"The locks aren't accessible from this side," said Cinnabar. "And the vents are too small for any of us to fit through."

"Are the hinges exposed?"

She nodded. "Yes, but they're sealed. It's not like we could pull the pins out."

"The ceiling is solid concrete." Max rapped a knuckle on the cold steel floor. "And we won't be tunneling either. So what does that leave?"

Simon reached into his pocket and plucked out a small package, which he held up. "Gum," he said.

"Gum?" Max echoed.

His father shook loose a couple of sticks and passed them to Max and Cinnabar. "Luckily, the bullyboy who searched me hadn't seen this before."

"Did he grow up on Neptune?" said Max, unwrapping his stick. "Everybody knows what gum is."

"Not this gum," said Simon. "It's an experimental prototype—very hush-hush. A mate of mine in Shanghai sent it along."

"Mmm, cherry," said Cinnabar, who'd popped her gum into her mouth and was chewing vigorously.

Simon raised a warning hand. "Careful. It's got a bit of a kick."

Cinnabar's eyes went round as saucers, and she spat the wad into her palm. "How's it work?"

"First, we need a spot of privacy." Simon chomped his own gum, then stood on his cot. By stretching to his full height, he was able to place the chewed-up lump over the security camera's lens. "With any luck, they'll think we're merely being difficult."

Max munched on his own stick of gum, removed it from his mouth, and squinted at it. "Okay, it can disable a camera. Anything else?"

His father smiled a roguish smile. "Wait and see. Why don't you and Cinnabar put your gum on the door hinges?"

They did as he suggested.

"Now take your wrapper and rub it between your fingers, hard and fast, like this." Simon demonstrated. "It's friction paper."

The wrapper quickly heated up in Max's hand. "Brilliant!"

"And before long . . ."

Fsst! One end of the paper glowed red, then burst into flame.

"Ow!" Max nearly dropped it, but managed to keep hold.

"Quickly," said his father. "Before it burns out—"

"I've got it," said Max, who was practiced in playing with fire. "We touch the flame to our gum."

"Precisely."

Gingerly, Max set the flame against his wad as Cinnabar followed suit. "Ow! Couldn't they design a better fuse?"

"Probably," Simon said. "That's why it's a prototype. Now stand back."

They huddled on the far side of the chamber. With a high, keening sound, the gum began to bubble and darken. Then a faint pop as the bubbling stopped. And . . .

Nothing happened.

The thick metal door stood there, same as before, solid and immovable. The hinges appeared untouched, save for the clumps of used gum.

Simon pressed his fingertips to his temples.

"Sorry, Mr. Segredo," said Cinnabar. "Looks like your mate sent you a dud pack."

"But he swore it would work," Max's father muttered, half to himself.

A spark of anger lit up Max like a cheap firecracker. He crossed to the door and pounded a fist on it. "Stupid high-tech spy gum!"

With a groan of complaint, the heavy door sagged in its frame, snapped its locks, and crashed to the floor.

Max gaped.

Cinnabar's face lit up like a geezer's last birthday cake in an incredulous smile. "It worked!"

"Let's go," said Simon. "That's bound to draw some attention."

They rushed through the door-shaped hole in the wall, but at the sight of the second cell, Max pulled up short. "Got any more of that gum?" he asked.

"Why?" said Simon.

Max hooked a thumb at the door. "Addison Rook is in there. We can't just leave him—plus, busting him out would really tick off Mrs. Frost."

"Good enough reason for me," said Simon, digging in his pocket.

"Um, no need for explosives," said Cinnabar. She put her hand on the door and pushed, revealing an empty chamber.

"Huh," said Max. "They must have traded him already." He shook it off. "Come on!"

Together, they hurried down the short corridor, and into LOTUS's command center. A tan, stocky man with a face like an old boot stepped from around the computer bank, his pistol coming up.

"Oi, what the devil—?" he began.

Max, in the lead, karate-chopped the weapon from his grasp. Cinnabar staggered the agent with a roundhouse kick, and Simon put him down with a brutal combination of punches.

"Now that's what I call teamwork," said Cinnabar.

Simon retrieved the agent's gun and made for the weapons locker. "Arm yourself," he said, then seemed to reconsider. "With nonlethal weapons."

"That's what we were planning anyway," said Max. "But I thought you were all about the bang-bang?"

"Your Hantai Annie has a point," said his father. "Underage kids and firearms don't mix."

The sight of the locker jogged Max's memory. "Oh, by the way, keep your eyes peeled for a tiger."

"A tiger?" Max's father frowned.

"Frost has strange taste in pets."

Cinnabar grabbed some pepper spray and a couple of smoke bombs, and Max was following suit when something in the next locker caught his eye.

"Hello, beautiful," he said. There hung the jet pack, buffed and polished and good as new.

"Max, leave it." Cinnabar was hurrying toward the spiral staircase, a few steps behind Simon.

"Uh-uh. This one's got my name on it."

Max lifted the jet pack from its hook and hustled after them. He couldn't believe this escape was going so well. No hungry tiger stalking them—yet. Only one guard, and he'd been no challenge. Max allowed himself a glimmer of hope that he might actually escape this loony bin and reunite with the rest of his friends, that everything might be just as it was at the School for S.P.I.E.S., only better.

And then . . .

Two figures rounded the curve of the steps above. Dijon LeStrange, pistol in one hand, was leading Wyatt Jackaroo.

"And where do you think *you're* going?" the LOTUS agent drawled.

CHAPTER 19

THE JET-PACK GETAWAY

SIMON SEGREDO whipped his pistol up in a two-handed grip, and pointed it straight at Dijon's heart.

"Don't shoot!" cried Wyatt, holding out both palms. The LOTUS agent at his side made no move to raise her weapon.

"And why not?" asked Mr. Segredo.

"Yamero," said Dijon in a gruff voice that wasn't her own. "Is bad luck to shoot your friends."

Wyatt watched the astonishment bloom on their faces. Cinnabar's hand flew up to cover her mouth. Max rocked back on his heels. Wyatt knew they were both thinking that the LOTUS agent sounded exactly like . . .

"Hantai Annie?" said Cinnabar.

One side of the woman's mouth twitched. "Well, it's not Easter Bunny."

"What the—?" Mr. Segredo lowered his weapon, and Wyatt remembered how to breathe again.

Max gasped and struggled to speak. "But you—I thought—" And then, as if a whirlwind of feelings had swept him up, he rushed forward to greet her.

The orphanage director trotted down the last few steps and gathered Max into a bear hug. "I know," she murmured. "I know." Wyatt beamed at them. Absolutely nothing beat tearful reunions—not even dark chocolate Kit Kat bars.

Max and Annie held the embrace for a long moment, and then Cinnabar came in for her own hug. Max's voice went all warbly. "But how . . . how did you . . . ?" He touched his own face while staring at Annie's.

"Bonzer disguise, isn't it?" said Wyatt, joining them. "I nearly had a thrombo when she caught me creeping about. Thought I was in the soup, for sure."

"I can't believe it." Cinnabar gaped at Hantai Annie's face and touched a hesitant finger to the director's cheek. "You look exactly like her."

Simon peered at the latex Dijon mask. "That's Ellie Crow's work, isn't it?"

"Best in town," said Annie. "Now, no more questions. *Ikuzo*—we go!"

As they hustled upstairs, however, Max voiced another concern. "Your voice," he said. "I thought you couldn't speak English that well?"

The spymaster glanced back over her shoulder at him. "Did you now?" she said, in a note-perfect imitation of Dijon's snide tone. "Perhaps you forgot that I speak seven languages. Perhaps you forgot what my name means."

"*Hantai* . . . means 'opposite,'" said Wyatt. "Like you do the opposite of what people expect."

She smiled. "Exactly."

Wyatt gave the others a look that said, *See? I knew it all along.* But honestly, he'd been just as stunned as they when he learned the truth.

The group reached Mrs. Frost's office without encountering any bad guys or tigers. As Annie worked the statuette to close the secret passage (whose mechanisms Wyatt *really* wanted to examine), Cinnabar asked, "But how did you know about this?" She motioned at the section of floor sliding back across the hidden stairwell.

"Dijon is very talkative, when I ask her the right way," said Hantai Annie. "She in New York now. That lady, she lacks job satisfaction."

Simon clapped a hand onto Max's shoulder. "Not us, eh?"

"Not now, anyway," said Max.

Wyatt was tickled to see a warm smile unfurl across Max's face at his father's touch. Maybe the two of them had patched up their differences after all?

Then Max frowned. "Hang on. How long have you been disguised as Dijon?"

"All day," said Hantai Annie.

"Then . . . you Tased me!"

She shrugged a shoulder. "*Gomen*. I had to stay in character."

Max shook his head in bemusement. "Sometimes you can be a real pain in the—"

"So," Wyatt cut in, rubbing his hands together, "what now?"

Hantai Annie scrutinized them. "You my prisoners. Hide weapons and follow my lead."

"Agreed," said Mr. Segredo.

After they'd slipped their gear into pockets or waistbands (aside from the jet pack, which Max wore on his back), the spymaster produced three sets of handcuffs. "Attach one side, but fake the other," she said. Wyatt and the rest complied, then, after a quick peek through the door, she marched them outside and down the hall at gunpoint.

Aware that the cameras were watching, Wyatt acted the part of a captured agent, slumping his shoulders and dropping his gaze. But inside, he was buzzing like he'd swallowed a bucketload of fireflies. Could they really walk out of the mansion like this, right under Mrs. Frost's nose? A prickle itched between his shoulder blades at the sight of every camera they passed, but at least the Three Musketeers were reunited.

His shoulder bumped Max's. "Good to have you back, mate," he muttered.

Max hid a grin. "It's not totally awful."

"Just like old times," said Cinnabar. Despite her handcuffs and haggard air, this was the happiest Wyatt had seen her in ages.

At the bottom of the stairwell, they followed Hantai Annie's escape route—a different route, Wyatt was glad to see, from the one Simon had taken when breaking in. By now, it was past 10 p.m. Wyatt supposed that much of the staff had retired to their own evil flats and houses—wherever bad guys holed up when off duty. The thickly carpeted halls were as empty as a vampire's hand mirror.

Moving quickly but calmly, Hantai Annie guided them to a side entrance that overlooked a garden. Through the window, the hedges were lit like a museum exhibit. Mrs. Frost and her bullyboys were nowhere to be seen.

Could it really be this easy? Wyatt's life in foster care told him, not bloody likely.

And what do you know? Wyatt was right.

Hantai Annie slid her key card through the scanner, they stepped out the door, and they nearly bumped into the looming figure of Styx.

The huge man lowered his buzz-cut head and stared. "What are this lot doing out?" he growled.

"Orders," said Hantai Annie in her bored Dijon voice.

Wyatt chewed his lip. Would their bluff work?

"Where you taking them?" said Styx.

Annie jerked her head to the right in a vague manner. "Out back."

"To the cages? That's daft." Styx's thick hand came up to scratch his bull neck. "Whose orders?"

"All the way from the top," said Dijon/Annie. "You want to argue with the guv'nor, be my guest." She kept her face bland, her manner casual and cruel.

Styx scowled, peering between her and her captives, like he knew something was dodgy, but couldn't put his finger on it. "Your face looks funny," he said.

"That's rich, coming from someone who used to model for Halloween fright masks," sneered Annie-as-Dijon.

Mr. Segredo tensed, readying for action. Wyatt rubbed his sweaty palms on his pants legs. Would the turncoat agent buy their lie?

Drawn to the movement, Styx's eyes widened. "Here now, this one's got loose."

Too late, Wyatt realized he'd separated his hands to wipe his palms. The handcuffs dangled from one wrist. "Heh." He offered a nervous smile. "No worries. I'm supertrustworthy."

Styx's hand strayed to his holster, where it hung under his arm.

Before the spy could draw his weapon or shout an alarm, Max whipped out his pepper spray and gave Styx a full blast, squarely in the face.

"Gaack!" The bearlike man staggered backward, arms

raised for protection. Simon Segredo punched him in his undefended gut.

Then, in a lightning-fast sequence of kicks and strikes, Hantai Annie had Styx on the ground gasping for air. She crouched over him, eyes blazing.

"*Omae,*" she spat. "You always were slow learner."

"Ah—Annie?" coughed Styx. His pale skin went even paler.

"Night-night, *traitor.*" And with that, she punched him in the temple.

Styx's head lolled. He was out cold.

"Quickly," Mr. Segredo said, stepping forward. "Help me truss up this stonking great rhino and hide him."

Working together, they cuffed Styx hand and foot. It took all five of them to lug his limp form into the shadows behind a hedge.

"Whatever else he's been doing here," grunted Wyatt, "he sure hasn't skimped on meals."

"They'll be sounding the alarm soon," said Mr. Segredo. "We should—"

"*Wakatta,*" said Annie. "We go."

She took the lead, slipping along the hedge line, staying low. Wyatt was sure that LOTUS had plenty of cameras covering the grounds. They were, after all, an ultra-high-tech outfit. Idly, he wished that S.P.I.E.S. had as many fancy toys for him to play with.

From the other end of the property, dogs barked.

Max's eyes widened. "Let's get cracking," he said. "We don't want to meet up with Wynken and Blynken."

"I like dogs," said Cinn.

"Not *these* mutts," said Max. "They're more like killer whales with legs."

Annie picked up the pace, and now they were nearly trotting, past a fountain and across a wide swath of lawn. At the rear of the group, Wyatt kept glancing behind them, not wanting to be surprised by snapping jaws and white fangs.

The wind shifted, and a familiar odor teased his nose. The tang of wet hay, overlaid with a musky scent and the hint of something even stenchier.

Wyatt slowed. "That smell. I know I've smelled it before."

Taking his arm, Max hurried him along. "Yes, it's the smell of your dirty laundry. Let's pick up the pace."

"No," said Wyatt. "It reminds me of the circus."

"The circus?" Now Cinnabar slowed too. "Your fosters took you to the circus? I'm jealous."

"It's probably Mr. Schnickelfritz," said Max. To their blank looks, he replied, "Mrs. Frost's pet tiger."

Hantai Annie glanced back and saw they'd fallen behind. *"Isoge!"* she snapped. "Move it!"

The dogs' barking grew louder, deep and rough. These were not happy puppies. Wyatt, Max, and Cinnabar broke into a run, following the adults.

"Actually," Wyatt panted, "when I was a . . . little

ankle-biter, my gran . . . worked in the circus. I was so . . . good with lions and tigers, everyone . . . called me the Cat Whisperer."

"Are you a dog whisperer too?" asked Cinn.

"Sorry, no."

"Then get your skates on, mate," said Max, lengthening his stride.

Hantai Annie led them through a stand of trees. Wet leaves squished underfoot, and Wyatt slid, banging his knee on an unseen trunk. When they emerged from the other side of the grove, they fetched up against the brick wall—tall, forbidding, and topped with razor wire.

"I don't suppose you've got a spare ladder?" said Simon Segredo, glancing down the path.

Distant shouts echoed from the mansion. Sweat drenched Wyatt's brow. They were up a gum tree for sure; the alarm was well and truly raised. He checked out the wall. No friendly tree branches overhung it, no mini-trampolines waited patiently.

How would they make it over?

"This way," said Annie, dashing to the left. The other four followed in her wake, pounding along the path between wall and trees. Wyatt sincerely hoped the spymaster had a plan.

Just when he began to get a wicked stitch in his side, Hantai Annie called a halt. Wyatt didn't like the worried light in her eyes.

"What?" asked Mr. Segredo.

"*Doko da?*" Annie mused. "Where is it?"

"Where's what?" said Cinnabar.

The spymaster scowled. "Rope ladder," she said. "Should be here." As she dug in a pocket for her cell phone, a funny expression crept across Max's face.

"Half a tick." He patted the straps of his jet pack. "Why don't I just fly everyone over?"

"Max," said Mr. Segredo. "I'm not sure . . ."

Cinnabar eyed the jet pack dubiously. "On that? Didn't you say you crashed it in the command center?"

"Well, yeah," said Max. "But that was my first flight. I'm loads better now."

"Because of all the practice you've had since then?" Cinnabar cocked her head.

"Here, I'll prove it," said Max. "Wrap your arms around me. You'll be my first passenger."

She backed away. "No, thanks."

"Wyatt?"

On the phone, Hantai Annie was asking Mr. Stones about the rope ladder. Mr. Segredo had trotted farther down the path, looking for another way over. Wyatt noticed the dogs' barks had changed pitch, from a deep *woof-woof* to the sort of bellowing cry that hunting bloodhounds made in old prison-break movies. They were on the move.

"Beauty," said Wyatt. "Let's do it."

He stepped close and awkwardly clutched Max in a bear hug. They were best mates, but it still felt weird to grab a guy like this. Max craned his neck around to see the controls. "Okay," he said. "Blast off in . . . three . . . two . . . one!"

The jet pack's engines roared like angry surf on a reef. With a sudden jerk, they were airborne.

Wyatt's feet dangled. A laugh erupted from him. "Hey! You did it!"

"See?" cried Max. "I told you—"

Before his friend could finish that thought, Wyatt felt himself traveling more backward than upward.

And just like that, *wham!* His back slammed into the brick wall, he lost his grip, and he plummeted to the ground.

As he lay flat on the path, Wyatt woozily watched Max and his jet pack zip back in the other direction, straight into a spreading oak tree.

"Baka yarou!" barked Hantai Annie. "Stop playing foolish!" She helped Wyatt stand and made sure he was okay.

"I'm not playing!" said Max, trying to disengage himself from a branch as the jet pack whined. He bobbed up, down, and around, like a hooked marlin fighting a fishing line. "I'm trying to—*ungh!*" With a last jerk, he wrenched himself free and whirled back into the air.

"Careful, Max!" cried Mr. Segredo, rejoining the group.

At that instant, floodlights flashed on, bright as a Barbados sunrise. Wyatt blinked, temporarily blinded. Shouts rang from behind them and from the right, as if two teams of guards were converging on the escapees.

"There!" cried Cinnabar.

When Wyatt's vision cleared, he saw what she was talking about: a heavy carpet had been tossed atop the razor wire. It was followed by the *whump* of a rope ladder being flung across the wall.

"Bloody thing!" Mr. Stones cursed from the other side.

Wyatt noticed that the ladder had missed the carpet entirely and now dangled across razor wire. He sure didn't fancy climbing that.

Stones tugged from the other side, but the rope was stuck fast. The team couldn't escape until their route was secure.

"Max-*kun*!" cried Hantai Annie. "Some help?"

CHAPTER 20

S.P.I.E.S.: ONE, LOTUS: NIL

IN THE GLARE of the floodlights, Max's golden-brown face seemed a little green around the gills. He wrestled with the jet pack's controls, first soaring too high, then nearly impaling himself on a wall spike.

"Watch it!" yelled Mr. Segredo.

Cinnabar's heart tried to crawl out of her throat. Would brave, reckless Max kill himself trying to save them?

At last, he managed to hook a foot under the ladder and lift it straight up, off the barbed wire. With a kick, he flipped it over so it lay on the protective carpet.

"Go, go, go!" cried Annie.

Wyatt leaped for the ladder and scrambled up the rungs.

"Whatever happened to ladies first?" Cinnabar asked.

"Sorry," called Wyatt over his shoulder. "Like I told you, I'm a cat person, not a dog person." Deep baying from the approaching watchdogs underlined his remark.

An amplified voice boomed from concealed speakers. "It's useless to run." Mrs. Frost's clipped, sneering tone was instantly recognizable. "My team will be on you in seconds— you can't escape."

"Just watch us!" shouted Max, and he spiraled like a dizzy butterfly, right over the wall and out of sight.

"You'd better not damage my jet pack!" snapped the LOTUS chief.

Cinnabar shook her head as she followed Wyatt up the ladder. "Too late."

At the top of the wall, she glanced back. Her stomach churned. A half-dozen LOTUS agents were racing down the pathway, around the bend. In seconds, they would spot Mr. Segredo, covering their backs, and Hantai Annie, who had just stepped onto the lowest rung.

"Enemy agents!" she called down, pointing at the onrushing spies.

Mr. Segredo brought up his pistol and squeezed off three shots as the first LOTUS agents hove into view. A couple of the spies ducked behind tree trunks to return fire while the rest crashed into the brush.

"They're circling behind you," Cinnabar cried.

One of the enemy agents shouted, "The brat on the wall is spotting for them."

"Take her out!" cried another.

A bullet whined, pinging off the iron spike beside Cinnabar. At the near miss, her innards turned to custard.

"Down!" cried Hantai Annie. *"Ijoge!"*

"Gladly," muttered Cinnabar, swinging her legs over the other side. The last thing she saw was Hantai Annie pitching a smoke bomb toward the shooter.

Rough hands helped her down the last rungs.

"All right, then, sunshine?" Mr. Stones's brown skin blended into the shadows, but his smile gleamed, a jack-o'-lantern grin.

"Never better," she said, giving him a quick hug.

Cinnabar noted that Tremaine and Nikki were helping disentangle Max from a gorse bush, mostly unharmed. "What about Annie and Mr. Segredo?"

"Don't worry your head about it, pumpkin cake. They're aces." Stones scowled. "What I'd give to be with 'em, handing those dirty buggers a bit of what-for, but the boss said to keep you lot safe."

A crafty look crossed his face. "Still, maybe I could lend a hand." The short, burly agent fished a smoke bomb from his jacket pocket. He cocked an arm to hurl it, but winced at the pain. "Bugger and blast!"

"Here, let me," said Cinnabar.

Grimacing, Mr. Stones passed over the device. "The shoulder's not quite up to snuff since I got shot. Bloody Styx—if I ever get my hands on that ratbag . . ."

"Right now he's knocked out and handcuffed."

Stones's smile returned. "That's my girl."

Cinnabar chucked the smoke bomb over the wall in the

same direction Hantai Annie had thrown hers, narrowly missing the spymaster's head as it popped into view. Hantai Annie merely grunted and dodged. She swung one leg over the carpet and, producing a pistol, lay down a covering fire for Mr. Segredo.

"I thought you didn't like guns," Cinnabar called up.

"I don't," said Annie. "Last resort only."

In another few seconds, Mr. Segredo's head poked up over the wall. He scrambled over and down, and then, after a few parting shots, Hantai Annie followed.

With Mr. Segredo's help, Stones yanked the rope ladder back over to their side of the wall. Working swiftly, they bundled it up.

"Think you're a bright spark, do you?" a deep voice boomed from the other side. Ebelskeever.

"Only compared to you," called Max. Wyatt snickered. It was childish, yes, but Cinnabar felt a chuckle bubbling up.

"You'll never stop us," snarled Ebelskeever. "You're just a blip. A bug on the windscreen."

"Yeah? Well, bug *this*," cried Nikki, tossing a flashbang in the direction of the voice. Curses and coughing followed the explosion, and Nikki grinned hugely.

"S.P.I.E.S.: one; LOTUS: nil," said Tremaine, bumping fists with her.

After the rescue, the team retreated to its run-down safe house above the Chinese restaurant, arriving seconds before the skies released a downpour. They sprawled on couches and chairs in the living room, digging into last night's leftovers with a vengeance.

"Missions always make me hungry," said Stones, popping a cold spring roll into his mouth.

"*Everything* makes me hungry," said Tremaine.

The reunited team members caught up on all that had happened during their separation. Cinnabar learned that Jazz was safe with Madame Chiffre, Miss Moorthy, and the rest of the gang, in temporary quarters not far from their old orphanage. In fact, the two sisters even got to talk with each other on the phone, laughing through tears.

It was bittersweet to know they'd have to stay apart awhile longer. But Cinnabar took comfort in knowing that Jazz was far safer where she was than here with them, going up against enemy spies.

She was also relieved to learn that Rashid was doing well in the hospital—well enough that he was complaining about missing out on the action.

When Max shared the story of his semi-undercover life at the LOTUS mansion, the mood turned serious. Even Nikki left off her usual needling when she heard the scope of LOTUS's plans.

"So, near as you can tell, they plan to use that brainwashing device on government ministers?" asked Mr. Segredo. His long face was as grim as a Christmas card from death row.

"Hard to say for sure," Max admitted. "But after seeing that layout of Parliament and the list of names on their computer, well, that's my best guess."

Cinnabar chewed on a fingernail.

Hantai Annie leaned back in her armchair and rubbed a hand over her jaw. She spoke the question that was on everyone's mind: "But why?"

Stones's eyebrows rose. "There's a lot—*mmph.*" He finished chewing his bite and gulped it down. "A lot you can do with the government of a major country in your pocket."

"Cause wars," said Tremaine.

"Drain the treasury," said Mr. Segredo.

"Pass a bill outlawing chocolate," said Wyatt. When everyone stared at him, he turned his palms up. "Hey, I wouldn't put it past them."

Steepling her fingers, Hantai Annie mused. "*Dame da.* Too much power in the wrong hands. We must stop them."

"But how?" asked Max.

Nobody answered.

For a while now, Cinnabar had been quiet, absorbing the situation and mulling over the events of the rescue mission. Something she'd heard earlier that night came back to her.

"What about your information?" she asked Mr. Segredo.

"How's that?" he said. In that moment, his warm brown eyes looked so much like Max's.

"Back at the mansion, you said you had evidence of LOTUS's crimes."

"Ripper!" Wyatt sat forward. "So we hand it to the cops or MI5, and Bob's-your-uncle, they lock up the bad guys."

"Bob's-your-uncle?" Max raised an eyebrow.

"My gran used to say that," said Wyatt. "She's been on my mind lately."

"Bob or no Bob"—Mr. Segredo unfolded his long legs to stand and pace—"it's not as easy as all that."

"Why not?" asked Stones, spearing a dumpling with a fork.

Stopping beside the front window, Mr. Segredo was back-lit by a red-and-yellow neon glow from the restaurant below. "For one thing, they've got contacts inside all of the major law enforcement agencies, people watching and waiting to snatch anything incriminating before it gets into the wrong hands."

"And for another?" asked Cinnabar.

"I fear the evidence may not be quite strong enough to lock them up for good. If that's the case, Mrs. Frost and her crew would be out on bail in a blink, protected by the best lawyers in the country." Mr. Segredo sighed, and in the lines of his face, Cinnabar saw the toll that living on the run had taken on him.

Hantai Annie spoke, her ebony eyes glittering. "So we must . . ." she said, "*nan to iu ka na?*—how you say? Catch them in the act."

"Brilliant," said Nikki, clapping her hands together. Her brow furrowed. "And just how do we do that?"

"Yeah, mon," said Tremaine, speaking up for the first

time, after snarfing a prodigious amount of moo shu pork. "Not to be a killjoy, but we're outnumbered and outgunned. LOTUS has a small army of spies, and we've only got what's in this room."

That sobering thought let some of the air out of their tires. Cinnabar sagged on the ratty sofa. How on earth would they pull this off?

Then Wyatt's blue eyes lit with a fiery light. His voice was low and intense, a Wyatt she hadn't seen before. "Did the French Resistance worry about that when they fought the Germans?" he said. "Did those three hundred Spartans worry about that when they went up against those other guys? Did Luke Skywalker worry about that when he struggled against the Empire?"

"Um, you know that last one's fictional?" said Max.

Shooting to his feet, Wyatt smacked his palm with a fist. "I tell you, we can do it!"

"What's gotten into him?" said Nikki.

"Too much hot mustard?" said Tremaine.

"Not quite." Cinnabar smirked and raised a spring roll in her chopsticks. "I think our boy may have an idea."

CHAPTER 21

GUERRILLAS IN THE MIST

NO SURPRISE, Wyatt's plan involved a fair amount of computer hacking. The S.P.I.E.S. crew split into two teams, drawing and redrawing their plans far into the night. Approaching the challenge from both ends, one group covered the government angle, and one tackled LOTUS.

Priority One became learning when LOTUS would make their move on the ministers. Simon Segredo and his team set to work trying to hack the government's database, searching for any mention of meetings with Mrs. Frost or LOTUS Security Systems, the spy agency's cover company. Wyatt's team had the unenviable task of hacking LOTUS's computer network, which was even better protected than the government's.

Max knew he was rubbish at computer hacking and strongest at fieldwork, so he and Hantai Annie elected to run a guerrilla campaign against LOTUS. He had no illusions. It was a little like trying to bring down a rogue elephant with a BB gun, but anything that harassed and distracted the enemy would work to their advantage.

Early the following morning, while the rest of the group slumbered in armchairs, sofas, and beds, Hantai Annie shook Max awake.

"Wuzza?" he mumbled.

"*Oi okiro!*" she said. "Wakey-wakey. Time to go."

He yawned hugely, sat up on his couch, and looked around. First light brushed the dark sky with a hint of pearl gray across the horizon. Cinnabar lay sprawled in the armchair beside him, soft and vulnerable in sleep, a strand of hair stuck to the corner of her mouth. Max felt the urge to reach over and pull it free.

"Well? You waiting for engraved invitation?" whispered Hantai Annie.

"Huh?" muttered Max. "Oh. I'm coming. Five minutes."

Ten minutes later, he trailed Annie out the door, still yawning. The chilly morning air helped rouse him, and by the time they reached the subway carrying pastries, tea, and heavily sugared coffee from a nearby bakery, Max felt nearly awake.

"So what's our strategy?" he asked, munching on a chocolate croissant.

Hantai Annie Wong patted the gear bag slung over her

shoulder. "Today, we take fight to them, like David and Goliath."

His forehead crinkled. "You know about that Sunday school stuff? I thought you were Buddhist or something."

"Even Buddhists like a good story." She winked, which was a little unnerving, like seeing a marble statue scratch itself. This lady was full of surprises.

After they boarded the train and got settled, Max recalled something he hadn't had time to pursue in all the excitement of the rescue operation.

He sent her a sidelong glance. "Can I ask something?"

"Mochiron," she said. "Ask away."

"Back at the mansion, when you were imitating Dijon, you spoke perfect English."

"Hai." She nodded.

"So . . . now you're back to talking like you always do," he said. "Why?"

"A woman has her secrets, and a spy woman has even more."

He rolled his eyes and shifted his body away, thinking, *I might have known not to expect a straight answer.* But after a sip of tea, she continued.

"The truth? To keep people off balance, but also . . ."

"Yes?"

"When you play a part long enough, it becomes part of you." Her eyes searched his. *"Wakatta ka?"*

Max swallowed, thinking of his time in the LOTUS mansion, spent pretending to be on their side. How he'd— even if only for a millisecond—considered the devil's bargain Mrs. Frost had offered. A light chill juddered across his shoulders.

"Now I have question for you," she said.

Max shrugged. "Okay."

"How are you?"

He flapped a hand, glancing away again. "Fine."

Annie reached over and gently turned his face toward her. "No. How are you *now*? You suffered much, Max-*kun*. You lose everything, and pretend to become what you hated. This would break many people."

Trying for a smile, Max found his bottom lip trembling. His voice wobbled. "Lucky thing I'm not most people."

She held his gaze for several heartbeats. "Lucky thing," she said. Annie squeezed his shoulder. "You good boy, Max-*kun*."

Max's throat constricted, and his eyes felt suspiciously misty, so he took another sip of coffee and rummaged around in the sack.

"I'm just glad we're all back together," he mumbled, thinking that he'd never spoken truer words. Max had to shake his head, marveling over how much had changed in a day.

Hantai Annie sent him a shrewd look. "Your father?"

Max stared down into the bag. "I almost can't believe it. You know?"

"*Wakatta*," she said.

"Do you think—can I . . . trust him?" Max almost hated to ask, but he needed to know her opinion.

For a stretch, the spymaster remained silent, considering. "He loves you," she said. "And he tries to change for you. Is *muzukashii*—very difficult. Real question is: Can you forgive him?"

Now it was Max's turn to ponder. "I . . . I'm getting there," he said at last.

"Like I say, you good boy."

By the time they reached the LOTUS mansion, the sun was struggling to pierce the blanket of low clouds that smothered the city. The rubbish collectors rattled up the street in their truck, leaving a cloud of acrid exhaust smoke in their wake, but all the residents were still indoors.

Annie tugged a baseball cap low over her face, and Max pulled the hood of his sweatshirt forward. "You know key to effective guerrilla warfare?" she asked.

"Surprise?"

One side of her mouth curved upward. "That, and don't get caught."

Max dug into his rucksack and came out with a small plastic box. "I know how I'm starting our campaign." Using the rubbish truck as cover, Max slipped past the mansion's driveway and scattered the entire box of tacks in the mud puddle that had pooled where driveway met street.

Making sure she was out of the security cameras' range, Hantai Annie tossed a few flash drives and CDs over the wall. Max smirked. "That'll hit 'em where it hurts," he said. "Someone will slip on those and fall on his bum."

Annie arched an eyebrow. "Wyatt's idea," she said. "Trojan horse program."

"Ah," said Max. "So if an agent finds one and puts it into his computer . . ."

Her hand darted out, imitating a striking snake. "Instant hack."

Max chuckled. "Clever boy, our Wyatt."

For the next few hours, they disabled security cameras, planted long-range listening devices in various trees, short-circuited the current in the wall-top razor wire, tossed hamburger balls laced with sleeping pills for the dogs, and generally made a nuisance of themselves.

Several times, guards rushed out to catch them, but each time Max and Annie melted away into the neighborhood. Once, a black Mercedes blasted down the driveway in pursuit and instantly got four flat tires on the hidden tacks. Humphrey, the driver, cursed so hard and so much, he grew light-headed and nearly passed out.

So this was guerrilla warfare.

Max loved it.

But more than that, he loved being back with Hantai Annie. He hadn't fully realized how much he'd missed her, and how concerned he'd been about her disappearance.

They capped off the morning's mischief by flagging down a grocery delivery truck that was pulling up to the gate. Annie had doffed her overcoat to reveal the black-and-silver uniform she'd worn as Dijon.

"Beg pardon," she said to the driver, a chubby man with a huge red walrus mustache.

He stopped the truck. "Yes?"

"I'm frightfully sorry, but there's been a change of plans," said Annie in a pretty good upper-crust accent.

Red Walrus frowned. "Oh?"

"Mrs., er . . ." She rotated a hand.

"Cheeseworthy," Max supplied.

"—has sent us out to catch you. It seems we've made a duplicate order for groceries. So sorry, but you'll have to take this load back."

"Take it . . . back?" The driver's face screwed up like he'd bitten into a bitter lemon. "The whole load?"

"That's right," said Annie. "If you bring this truck through those gates, Mrs. Cheeseworthy will be . . . what's the phrase?"

"Seriously cheesed off," said Max with a straight face.

Red Walrus's eyes widened.

"You don't want to cheese off the cook, do you?" said

Hantai Annie in her gravest tones. "She might pull all her business away from your store. It's happened before."

Max could scarcely contain his laughter at the expression on the man's face.

"No," said Red Walrus. "Heavens no. Thanks for the warning, ma'am."

"Not at all," she said. "Be seeing you."

The portly man reversed his truck and drove away without another word. Max burst out laughing. Even Hantai Annie cracked a tiny smile.

"Army runs on its stomach," she said. "And this army will be *hara hetta*—very hungry."

Shaking his head in admiration, Max said, "You're devious."

"You are too kind," said Annie. She jerked her head to the side. "*Owatta*. We leave now."

"Already?" said Max.

She cast a glance at the mansion. "By now, everyone is awake and active. Remember second key of guerrilla warfare?"

"Don't get caught," Max said.

"Maybe we return tonight," said Annie. "For more fun. But now we meet with member of House of Lords."

Max frowned. "Someone from Parliament? What for?"

"To show us how to break into government building, of course."

◊ ◊ ◊

A short while later, Max and Hantai Annie joined the line outside the public entrance to the Houses of Parliament, a colossal limestone structure on the riverbank. Eager students and foreign tourists kept up a babble of conversation as the line inched forward.

Unlike their fellow visitors, Max and Annie had zero interest in the collections of art, the historical structures, or the intricate workings of government. They were probing for weak spots in the security system.

Max noted the stern-faced policemen posted seemingly everywhere, surveying the crowd with suspicious eyes. As he and Hantai Annie passed through security, he registered the metal detector, the X-ray scanner, and the care the cops took in screening everyone. When a constable confiscated the penknife on a teacher's key ring, Max leaned close to Annie and whispered, "How in the world could LOTUS smuggle the brainwashing device past all this?"

Hantai Annie's mouth tightened. "Never worry. They find a way."

Reading the posted list of banned items—pepper spray, knives and other sharp objects, climbing gear, spray paint— Max was glad they'd left Annie's bag of tricks in a locker at the tube station. Shame to lose such useful equipment.

While researching this government complex online, Hantai Annie had learned that it had witnessed a fair amount of theft over the years, as well as the odd protest action. Articles had mentioned all these things, but neglected to state the most important detail: how the thieves and pro-testors broke in.

Max mused. This was the government's nerve center. If the cops couldn't even prevent thievery, how could they forestall a much more serious threat?

After collecting their security lanyards at the check-in desk, Max and Annie joined a small group waiting in an alcove. Right on time, a tall, pale woman with a beaky nose and the predatory look of a wading bird stalked up to them, trailed by a much shorter Indian man. He scooted around her to address the cluster of people.

"Welcome, welcome!" he said. "The eleven o'clock tour for Lady Sallow-Dankworth? I'm Kevin Chopra, and this, of course, is her ladyship."

Lady Sallow-Dankworth stared down her considerable nose at the group, and seeing those nostrils, Max whim-sically wished for a Plexiglas shield in case she sneezed. "Greetings to all of you," she began, in a voice that seemed to emerge from somewhere deep in her sinuses. "And wel-come to the place where it all happens, the very epicenter of—" Her gaze fell upon Hantai Annie, and the lady visibly blanched. "Er, your government," she concluded.

The spymaster showed the politician a serene expression.

"I shall leave you in Mr. Chopra's capable hands," the lady said. "As I have, er, pressing business to attend to."

Another nervous glance at Hantai Annie. "We do hope you enjoy your tour."

"Right this way, please, ladies and gents," said Kevin. "You'll discover that lawmaking is rather like sausage making—once you learn the process, you may find you've lost your appetite." Dutiful laughter followed his remark.

As the tour group shuffled off, Max muttered to Annie, "Is she afraid of you?"

"Let's say she owes me," said the spymaster.

At last the band moved out of earshot. With a quick glance to either side, Lady Sallow-Dankworth approached.

"Whatever is the matter?" she whispered. "I left a very important budget meeting for this."

"*Hisashiburi,*" said Hantai Annie. "Good to see you too."

Belatedly, the politician seemed to recall her manners and stuttered a brief greeting. Max couldn't help observing that this woman really didn't want to be in Hantai Annie's debt.

"Problem is this," said Annie. "A powerful group wants to control your government. We believe they will make their move in the next few days." In brief terms, she sketched out what they had learned about the threat from LOTUS.

At the mention of a mind-control device, Lady Sallow-Dankworth brayed a laugh that sounded more like a donkey than one would have expected from such a birdlike woman. "Brainwashing? You pulled me out of a vital meeting to discuss some science-fiction threat?"

Hantai Annie bristled, but her voice stayed steady. "No science fiction; fact. People have died for this invention, and if LOTUS gets to use it on—"

"I've been very patient with you," said the politician, "but if you expect me to take such a ridiculous claim to the security department, you don't know Lady Sallow-Dankworth. Why, I'd be laughed out of the building. My reputation—"

"*Baka yarou,*" snapped Hantai Annie. "Reputation will not help if you are puppet of LOTUS."

The lady waved her hand as if brushing away a fly. "No, no, no. Mrs. Wong, I owe you a great debt, but I simply cannot involve myself with this matter."

A muscle jumped in Hantai Annie's jaw. "Let me talk to security chief and learn the building's vulnerable spots."

The politician shook her head.

"At least tell us if ministers are meeting with LOTUS Security Systems."

"Dreadfully sorry, but even if I knew it, that's restricted information." Lady Sallow-Dankworth kept shaking her head back and forth like a metronome. "Now, that's all the time I can spare. You may join the tour or you may leave—entirely your choice."

A sudden idea struck Max. "Can I at least use the toilet before we go?" he asked in his most innocent voice.

The politician tilted her head back, sighed as if she were

doing him a huge favor, and pointed to the nearby loo. Max trotted off.

Pushing his way inside, he winced at the pungent smell of antiseptic cakes and urine, and immediately started assessing the chamber as a hiding place. No security cameras or alarms that he could see. Loads of stalls. There was even a spacious janitor's closet with a lock that could be easily jimmied.

He surveyed the room with a satisfied smile. Stinky, but it would serve.

"I say, young fellow," said a stuffy-looking man staring at Max from a stall doorway. "What precisely are you doing here?"

"Research," said Max.

A furrow appeared between the man's eyebrows. "Research?"

"For my, er, blog," said Max with a disarming smile. "Top Ten Loos of the Land. I'd say this one is number three with a bullet—wouldn't you agree?"

Gawking at Max like he'd just sprouted a third eyeball on his forehead, the man edged around him and hurried outside without even washing his hands.

Max rejoined Hantai Annie, who was pacing her corner of the great hall and scowling at any officials who happened by. "Fools," she muttered. "Not smart enough to save themselves."

He lifted a shoulder. "Did you expect any different?"

Stopping her pacing, Annie narrowed her eyes. "No. But this is why I don't work for government intelligence."

"Government *intelligence?* That's one of those contradiction thingies," said Max as they headed for the exit. "Like easy algebra or jumbo shrimp."

"Oxymoron," said the spymaster.

Now it was Max's turn to narrow his eyes. "I keep forgetting. Your English is better than you let on."

A slight twitch of her mouth was Hantai Annie's only response.

CHAPTER 22

BIG HACK ATTACK

BACK AT THE SAFE HOUSE above the Chinese restaurant, Wyatt was doing the happy dance. "Because I'm *bad*, I'm *bad*, I break a bum-da-dum-dum," he sang as he tried to imitate moves he'd seen on TV.

"I'll say." Nikki looked up from her laptop computer. "If you're gonna butcher a song, at least get the lyrics right," she groused.

Wyatt was in such a good mood, not even Nikki could burst his bubble. "Aw, you're just brassed off because you're still hunting for a back door, while I've hacked the LOTUS private network." He strutted around the takeout-strewn living room, waving his arms in what he was almost sure was a hip-hop move. "I am the King Kong champion of all hack—*ow!*"

"Enough!"

The happy dance came to an abrupt end when Nikki grabbed on to his ear and twisted. Okay, so maybe he wasn't *quite* in the sort of mood where Nikki couldn't bother him. Maybe that state didn't actually exist.

"Settle down, cupcake," growled Mr. Stones, separating the two of them.

"But he—" Nikki began.

The burly man cut her off. "Save your spleen for the enemy."

"Thanks," said Wyatt.

"Even if he *is* bloody annoying," continued Stones as if he hadn't heard, "Wyatt's on our side, remember."

The redheaded girl grumbled, but she sat back down.

"Let's see what you got, boy-o," said Stones to Wyatt. He came around to peer at the blond boy's laptop.

Still rubbing his smarting ear, Wyatt joined him. "See?" he said. "Someone must've picked up one of our Trojan horse thumb drives and plugged it into their computer."

Mr. Stones squinted at the screen and rubbed his unshaven jaw, producing a sound like sandpaper on a wall. "Well, paint me pink and call me Mary. What am I seeing here?"

"Some kind of message from the system admin," said Wyatt.

"Then why's it look like alphabet soup gone through a blender?"

"Um, well, it's still encoded," said Wyatt. "But I've got

three decryption programs working on cracking it."

"Yeah, *who's* bad?" Nikki smirked.

"I need more tea and bikkies," mumbled Wyatt.

Stones clapped him on the back as he shuffled off toward the kitchen. "Good job, sunshine. We're gettin' there. At least you broke in."

Wyatt stretched and yawned. They'd been at it nonstop for six hours, ever since he woke up this morning—one team in the living room, one team in the master bedroom—hacking away for all they were worth. Searching for the information that this mission depended on. His breakthrough was the first, but now that the balloon of his excitement had been punctured, Wyatt realized it could easily be another six hours before his software broke the LOTUS code.

He hoped it would be in time. Wyatt had a bad feeling that Mrs. Frost would use her dangerous new toy sooner rather than later.

And he really didn't want to witness the results.

Switching on the heat under the kettle, he dumped the old tea leaves into the sink and added some fresh Earl Grey to the brewing basket.

"Any progress?"

Wyatt wheeled about to see Cinnabar enter the kitchen. "Oh, I cracked LOTUS's private network," he said in what he hoped was an offhand way. "You?"

"Wyatt, that's brilliant!" Cinn rushed over and grabbed him by both hands.

His cheeks warmed at her praise. "Yeah, well. It's all encoded anyway."

"Even so," she said. "Well done, you. We've been trolling the government Web sites for hours, and so far, nothing about LOTUS, and no luck with the hacking."

Wyatt's gaze dropped to the soggy tea leaves in the sink. "Cinn, what if we're too late?"

"What do you mean?"

That tickle of dread in the pit of his stomach sharpened. "They've got all the money, all the manpower, all the connections. What if we can't stop LOTUS in time?"

She gripped his hands tighter and gave Wyatt a little shake.

"We'll just have to, that's all," she said lightly. But the false cheer in her voice was as obvious as a preschooler's lie.

Mr. Stones called from the next room. "Wyatt? Get your bucket in here."

Wyatt's eyes met Cinnabar's, which were as mystified as his own. They hustled into the living room, where Stones and Nikki stood over Wyatt's laptop.

"Problem?" said Wyatt, joining them.

Stones only pointed.

On the screen, one of the deciphering programs had finally stopped its work. A pop-up message blinked in blue letters:

Type password and press ENTER for result.

With quivering fingers, Wyatt typed his password and tapped the key. Two lines scrolled across the screen:

Tonight's the night. 7:30 p.m.
A and B teams to Location I.

"Brilliant," said Cinnabar with a wide smile. "So where's Location One?"

If the shabby safe house had been a beehive of activity earlier, this news amped things up to a whole new level. While Wyatt continued to search for and decode other LOTUS messages, the rest of the crew set their sights on pinning down Location I.

With only six and a half hours to go, this task took on a certain urgency.

Stones and Mr. Segredo barked orders, hurrying back and forth between computers and phoning all their contacts for leads. Tremaine, Cinnabar, and Nikki hacked for all they were worth. Hantai Annie and Max were headed back in, Max having managed to scatter a few more of Wyatt's Trojan horse drives in Parliament's employee parking lot.

Everyone focused on that seven thirty deadline. Everyone tried to discover where the meeting would take place.

Had LOTUS lured the top ministers with a conference on some vital topic—national security, perhaps? Wyatt wondered. Or was Mrs. Frost's group planning to crash some other gathering that had already been slated?

No seven thirty ministerial meetings of any sort showed up on the publicly accessible schedules. But many sensitive discussions weren't listed. Despite pleas, complaints, and veiled threats, the offices of Mr. Stones's and Mr. Segredo's MPs were of no help whatsoever.

Through it all, Wyatt was impressed at how well Max's dad was able to work with the rest of the S.P.I.E.S. team. For a lone wolf and man of mystery, he displayed surprising patience and an ability to operate within the group. True, Mr. Segredo and Stones occasionally had their differences, but so far they'd been able to iron things out without having to resort to biting and punching.

At last, Hantai Annie arrived with Max in tow, and everyone crowded around them, talking at once.

"Director, there's only five hours left!"

"Come and see what we did with LOTUS's e-mail system."

"I can't work with Nikki any longer—she's driving me bonkers!"

Hantai Annie held up a hand. *"Oi! Shizukani shiro!"* she barked. "Everybody shut you mouth!"

Finally, the living room fell silent.

"One at a time, make report."

Taking turns, the team members filled her in on their

progress. After a brief huddle with Stones and Mr. Segredo, Hantai Annie addressed the group.

"Time is short, and we don't know location," she said. "So we play odds."

"Play odds?" asked Max. "Like with horse racing?"

"*Atari*," she said. "You got it. Odds are, meeting is somewhere in Parliament. So, we keep searching for site, but we prepare for meeting to happen there. *Wakatta ka?*"

"Loud and clear," said Tremaine.

"No time to plan fancy break-in," said Hantai Annie.

Stones screwed up his face thoughtfully. "How about staging a diversion?"

"No good," said Mr. Segredo. "One whiff of any threat, and the whole place goes into lockdown."

Mr. Stones shot him a dirty look, but said nothing.

"So, how do we get inside?" asked Wyatt.

Hantai Annie arched an eyebrow. "Only way a group of kids can get in," she said. "School tour."

AN ALARMING TOUR

IT TOOK some quick scrambling and a fair amount of arm-twisting on Lady Sallow-Dankworth (not literal arm-twisting, though Annie was sorely tempted), but in the end, the Merry Sunshine Orphanage School was able to arrange a last-minute parliamentary tour at four fifteen that same day.

Now all they had to do was sneak away from their guide, hack into the massively protected computer system of one of the world's most developed nations, and save that nation's government from a diabolical plot—all by seven thirty that night.

No pressure there, thought Cinnabar.

There wasn't time to hunt down private-school uniforms before they left, for which Cinnabar was eternally grateful. (It's hard to rock a boring blue-and-gray outfit with dorky school tie, after all.) So instead, the S.P.I.E.S. crew ended up wearing street clothes and going as themselves—an unusual and uncomfortable situation for a group of spies.

Thanks to the security screening process, they had to leave nearly all weapons behind. Still, the group managed to smuggle a few useful items into the building. A bad moment came when the police challenged Mr. Stones's "cane," but when he loudly griped that he'd received his "injury" defending the country in the last war, the duty sergeant waved him through. At last, the team reached its appointed rendezvous and discovered Lady Sallow-Dankworth's aide, Kevin Chopra, waiting for them.

"Welcome to all you Merry Sunshine students and—" the Indian man began, and then he caught sight of Max and Annie. "Er, hang on. Didn't I see you two earlier?"

Max grinned and held up his palms. "Busted," he said. "We wanted to find out whether our school would enjoy the tour."

Cinnabar admired how he could turn on the charm like that, and it seemed to be working—mostly.

"But why did you book your tour at the last minute?" Mr. Chopra asked.

"Because . . ." Cinnabar lied, "our, um, mock Parliament debate is tomorrow, and we simply *must* see the real thing first." She gave him a dose of her own charm, batting those golden eyes that many said were her best feature.

Mr. Chopra's forehead creased. "Are you all right, miss? Something in your eye?"

Suppressing a flicker of irritation, Cinnabar assured him she was fine. Her charm might not have worked as intended, but at least it helped distract their guide from uncomfortable subjects.

"Everyone stay close, please," said the aide. "At this late hour, we may not be able to offer the full tour, but if we move smartly, we can hit at least some major highlights. This way to the Central Lobby."

Max leaned close to the spymaster. "I can't believe you got us in. Exactly what do you have on Lady Sallow-Dankworth?"

"Kept her son's story out of media," Annie whispered. Her index finger went to her lips in a *shush* gesture. "*Very* embarrassing."

As Mr. Chopra led them off, Hantai Annie gave a tiny nod to Cinnabar and Wyatt.

"Sorry, mate," said Wyatt, "but I need to make a pause for the cause."

The aide glanced around, frowning. "Beg pardon?"

"You know," said the blond boy, tilting his head toward the toilets. "See a man about a horse? Punish the porcelain? Drain the—"

"Yes, me too," Cinnabar cut in. "Don't worry, we'll catch up to you in the er, Main Lobby."

Mr. Chopra handed them a doubtful look, but Hantai Annie barked commands, hustling the little band forward, and she was a force of nature that few could resist. Cinnabar and Wyatt entered the respective ladies' and gents' rooms, waited for couple minutes, and then peeked outside.

The coast was clear. Their team had marched out of sight, and this late in the day, only a group of French tourists could be seen, making its way toward the exit.

Cinnabar jerked her head at Wyatt and mouthed, "Let's go."

Strolling casually, they headed along the hallway. A passing pair of constables glanced at them curiously, but didn't break stride or stop their conversation. When a narrow corridor appeared on the right, Cinnabar and Wyatt ducked into it.

"According to the map, there are loads of offices down this way," said Cinnabar. The air felt stale and musty, like nobody had ever opened any windows and people had been breathing the same oxygen over and over since Shakespeare's time. Everything smelled like old leather and dust.

"All we need is one open computer," said Wyatt. "Shouldn't be too hard this late in the day."

"Assuming Mr. Chopra doesn't come searching for us," said Cinnabar. "Or security doesn't get suspicious."

Wyatt cocked his head. "Well, aren't you just a ray of sunshine?"

She shot him a glare. Maybe she was being overly pessimistic, but Cinnabar couldn't shake a sense of unease. This spying mission carried serious consequences if they were caught.

Unlike the grander main passageway, this hallway seemed

narrow and dingy, designed to impress no one. Offices crowded together like shoe boxes on a hoarder's shelf. At the first few doors they startled a few secretaries who wondered aloud what kids were doing in this wing.

"Hunting for my dad's office," said Wyatt, employing his big-eyed, innocent-baby expression. "Sorry to trouble you."

Cinnabar was irked to see that his goofy brand of charm was more effective than hers. Not that they were having a charm competition or anything.

Finally, near the end of that long corridor, she and Wyatt came across the perfect candidate: an office that was both unoccupied and unlocked.

"You stand guard, I'll go hacking," said Wyatt.

"No, *you* stand guard, and I'll hack," said Cinnabar.

They glared at each other for a few beats, then simultaneously seemed to realize that their search time was limited.

Wyatt shrugged. "Okay, we'll both go in."

Once through the door, Cinnabar turned the bolt to give them a bit of warning, and Wyatt took advantage of her delay to scoot in front of the room's only computer.

"Hey!" she said.

"Snooze, you lose," he crowed, plugging a thumb drive into the USB port and beginning to work on cracking the password.

Cinnabar put her fists on her hips and blew out some air, considering. Time was tight; she couldn't waste it arguing with Wyatt. She'd have to be the mature one—like always.

Giving the cubbyhole-size office the once-over, she noted details: the stacks of papers piled on every horizontal surface, the dusty old fan, assorted keepsakes, and the many framed photos of the MP (a tired-looking blond man) smiling phony smiles with various other people in dark suits. On the wall above the MP's desk, a poster featuring a crowned vulture declared KEEP CALM AND CARRION.

Did people lose their sense of humor when they entered politics? Cinnabar wondered.

On the hunch that maybe not everyone kept their schedule on the computer, she rooted around the messy desk for a calendar or appointment book. No luck. She did encounter a cup of lukewarm coffee, stacks of complaint letters, an engraved invitation to some kind of event called Cirque du Chat that evening, and notes on a civil service committee meeting that were dull enough to put a sugar-crazed kindergartner to sleep in the blink of an eye.

The doorknob rattled.

"Thought you didn't lock up," said a male voice outside.

"Must have done it on autopilot," a female voice replied. The key scraped in the lock.

Cinnabar and Wyatt shared a worried glance. He pocketed the thumb drive. She scanned the tiny office. Nowhere to hide—they'd simply have to brass it out.

Waving Wyatt to the secretary's seat, Cinnabar took the

visitor chair, folded her arms, and assumed an expression somewhere between bored and annoyed. Inside, her heart thudded like a trip-hammer.

The door swung open to admit a slender gray-haired man with skin a shade darker than Cinnabar's, and a pale woman whose jerky movements reminded her of a chicken.

"*There* you are," said Cinnabar, rising from her chair. "We've been waiting to see our MP for *ages*, haven't we, Waldo?"

"*Mmm?*" said Wyatt, not realizing he was Waldo. "Oh, er, yes. Yes, we have, er, Cindy."

Gray Hair stepped in front of Chicken Woman, as if to protect her from the ferocious teens. "How did you get in here? It was locked."

Favoring him with a pitying smile, Cinnabar said, "I know. We locked it—for safety."

"Who are you?" he demanded.

"We're, um, constituents," said Wyatt.

Chicken Woman squinted at them. "But you're too young to vote."

"*Children* of constituents," Cinnabar corrected, "and we've been waiting donkey's years to talk to the MP about school funding."

"But we were only gone for a—" Gray Hair began.

Wyatt tossed up his hands. "Clearly he doesn't value our vote—er, our parents' vote." He stood, pretending to be upset.

Unfortunately, his acting wasn't good enough for a primary-school play, let alone the world of espionage.

"And after we came all this way too," said Cinnabar, joining Wyatt. She took on an offended tone. "I guess an appointment doesn't mean what it used to."

At the word *appointment*, Chicken Woman jerked her head around to stare at the computer. She bustled over to her keyboard. "You were on the schedule? I'll just check. . . ."

Cinnabar's breath caught in her throat. On the one hand, she wanted to peek at the MP's schedule. On the other hand, she wanted to flee, since she knew they weren't on it. Peeking won. She wandered a step closer and watched the screen as Chicken Woman scrolled up and down the MP's appointments.

"And your family name?" the assistant asked.

"Brixton," said Cinnabar, who'd always rather fancied the name. "Cindy and Waldo Brixton. We're, um, cousins," she said, forestalling questions on the differences in their hair and skin color.

"Brixton . . ." said the woman, searching through the schedule. "I don't see . . ."

And there—as Chicken Woman scrolled down far enough to reveal the evening's meetings, Cinnabar got what she came for. No official meetings at six, seven, or seven thirty. Either this MP wasn't on LOTUS's target list, or tonight's gathering was unofficial.

Bumping Wyatt with her shoulder, she edged toward the office door. "Ah, forget it. We've waited long enough, and now we have to go."

Gray Hair blocked their exit, arms crossed and wide mouth set in a frown. "You're not going anywhere until I hear some kind of reasonable explanation for your presence."

Uh-oh. The man was bigger than both of them, and although Cinnabar and Wyatt might be able to take him out with their martial-arts moves, security would take *them* out of the building.

They needed a distraction, and they needed it now.

The door swung open. "*There* you are!" chirped a jolly voice.

Stepping aside to see, Gray Hair revealed Simon Segredo standing in the doorway. The dapper spy wagged a finger good-naturedly. "I got worried when you wandered off."

"And you are?" Gray Hair scowled.

"Their father," said Mr. Segredo.

"Well, *my* father, anyway," Wyatt put in.

Chicken Woman's eyebrows squished together. "Mr., er, Brixton?"

With a lightning glance to Cinnabar for confirmation, Mr. Segredo said, "That's right. Sam Brixton Jr." His acting was *much* better than Wyatt's. "So," he addressed Gray Hair like an old school chum, "is your MP headed to that big meeting tonight?"

"Big meeting?" The man cocked his head.

"Sure. The one everybody's talking about?"

Gray Hair cocked his head the other way, like a befuddled beagle who's lost the scent. "Everybody?"

Mr. Segredo frowned playfully. "Ooh, sorry, old bean. Guess your guv'nor's not high enough up the food chain to wangle an invite."

"I—I beg your pardon?" Gray Hair didn't know whether to be offended or concerned.

Max's father flapped a hand. "Forget I even mentioned it. Come along, children—your mum is waiting."

As she and Wyatt sauntered past Gray Hair and out the door, Cinnabar couldn't resist a parting jab. "A shame about your MP. Guess that's what comes of not looking after school funding."

The man blinked rapidly, not entirely sure of what had just happened.

As they headed down the hall, Wyatt said, "Beauty move, Mr. S! That bloke didn't know whether to scratch his watch or wind his bum."

Max's father waved aside the compliment. "He also didn't know about our meeting. Did you two learn anything?"

"Nothing on the appointment calendar," said Cinnabar. She turned to Wyatt. "Tell me you got something from the computer."

"I'm a hacker, not that guy from *The Matrix*." Wyatt

scowled. "Didn't even have time to crack the password."

Mr. Segredo grimaced. "Hopefully we'll get another shot at it before the tour is over, or . . ." He didn't need to complete the thought. They all knew the consequences of failure.

Hurrying down another narrow corridor, they entered a room the likes of which Cinnabar had never seen before. It seemed entirely dipped in gold, from the diamond-shaped tiles on the floor, to the fancy filigree on the walls, to the chandeliers and the intricate ceiling above them. An enormous tapestry of something historical dominated one wall, while oil portraits of kings and queens glowered down from all around.

"Ah! I *told* you they show up soon," came Hantai Annie's voice. "And here they are."

Cinnabar whirled to see her classmates and teachers enter the long hall through a side entrance, accompanied by Kevin Chopra. The aide wore a nervous frown.

"Really, Mrs. Wong," he said. "They're not supposed to be roaming about unsupervised."

"They weren't unsupervised," said Mr. Segredo. "They were with me."

Wincing apologetically, Mr. Chopra said, "Still, I could land in a great deal of trouble for—"

Mr. Stones clapped the man on the shoulder. "Don't sweat it, Kev. No harm, no foul. Higgledy-piggledy-pop—they're back in a jiffy, and no one's the wiser."

The aide didn't look mollified, but he resumed his tour-guide spiel. From Max's and Nikki's expressions, Cinnabar judged that the S.P.I.E.S. team had had it with government and history, and was spoiling for some proper action.

As the group shuffled into the next room, Max fell behind, edging up to Cinnabar. "Well?" he muttered. "Happy hunting?"

She shook her head.

He grimaced. "And they're going to boot us out of here in less than half an hour. Time for Plan B."

"We have a Plan B?" said Wyatt.

"Always," said Max. "But we need to be closer to the loo for it to work."

"Oh," said Wyatt. "*That* Plan B."

Somehow, Cinnabar and her friends managed to grit their teeth and survive another fifteen minutes of Simon de Some-body's medieval parliament and the story behind the stained-glass windows. At last, Mr. Chopra led them on a meandering course back toward the hall where they'd entered.

When they neared the bank of toilets, a series of signifi-cant glances took place: Annie to Stones, Stones to Tremaine, and Tremaine to Max. Then Mr. Stones approached Kevin Chopra with a detailed question, maneuvering him so that his back was to Tremaine and Max. The older teen leaned against the wall by the fire alarm, blocking the view of the nearest security camera with his broad back.

Max casually propped himself by Tremaine, like they were sharing some juicy gossip. Then he brushed back the Plexiglas cover and pulled the switch.

Ning-ning-ning-ning-ning! keened the fire alarm, at a volume loud enough to give orbiting aliens a headache.

This part of the plan was easy. Like the rest of her crew, Cinnabar clapped her hands over her ears and screamed as they ran about like a flock of panicked turkeys. The aide tried unsuccessfully to corral his tour group, which had no intention of being corralled. In no time at all, a river of people streamed down the hall from deeper in the building, making for the exit.

Taking advantage of the cover, the S.P.I.E.S. team members slipped into either the gents' or ladies' toilets. Cinnabar was one of the last to hide, and as she ran into the loo, she nearly collided with a middle-aged woman running out.

The woman caught her arm and shouted something that was drowned out by the annoying alarm. Her grip was harder to break than a Chinese substitution code. When Cinnabar shook her head, making the I-can't-understand-you face, the woman pointed at her, then at the exit.

Cinnabar nodded, mimed really having to go to the toilet, and held up an index finger as if to say, *One minute.* The woman shook her head again and began leading her away from the loo. Cinnabar shrugged agreeably and accompanied her. When at last the Good Samaritan released her, Cinnabar slipped into the flow of people leaving the building and doubled back to the loo.

Unlike the men's toilet, which, according to Max, boasted a janitor's closet for easy concealment, this loo had none. *Thanks, Max.* After trying the first stall and finding it locked, Cinnabar entered the second cubicle. She barred the door, closed the toilet lid on some unspeakable mess, and squatted atop it to wait, trying to breathe through her mouth. She considered flushing, but didn't want the noise to reveal her presence.

The wail of the fire alarm kept up, like a wet baby seeking relief, for what seemed like ages. At last it cut off abruptly, midshriek.

"About bloody time," was the comment from the stall beside her. Nikki.

"*Shh!*" hissed Hantai Annie from the other side. "No noise!"

Through the metal partition, Cinnabar could picture Nikki's eyes roll, but the redheaded girl said nothing further.

Time passed. *Loads* of time.

The toilet door creaked open. "Anyone in here?" said a gritty female voice. "Hullo?"

A long pause, during which Cinnabar could hear breathing.

The door closed, and the woman went away.

It struck Cinnabar that eventually, the janitor would come

in to clean the toilets, and they had no idea when that might be. After hesitating several times, she shared this thought with Hantai Annie.

As it was already past five thirty, the spymaster agreed that it might be safer to hide in an empty office. After all, the team still had to locate the meeting where LOTUS would make their play. Moving as quietly as ants crawling on cotton, Cinnabar, Nikki, and Hantai Annie left their stalls and crept to the outer door.

The spymaster cracked it open just enough to peer outside.

"Okay," she said, after a long pause. *"Ikuzo."*

Cinnabar slipped out the door after Nikki and Annie.

"Freeze!" a rough voice barked. "Don't move a muscle."

CHAPTER 24

ALL LOCKED UP AND NOWHERE TO GO

AS MAX SOON DISCOVERED, the toilets *were* subject to surveillance after all. The cameras had simply been concealed behind mirrors so as not to make visitors uncomfortable. He learned this helpful fact from the constables hustling them into the police van.

"You film people in the loo?" squawked Max. "What kind of pervs are you?"

"The kind that like to keep our politicians safe," said one stone-faced cop.

Nikki punched Max's shoulder with her cuffed fists. "Thanks loads, Maxi-Pad."

Max protested, "It's not like we had time to properly check it out before we—"

"That'll do," said Simon, with a meaningful glance at the officer handcuffing him to a roll bar.

"Your father is right," said Hantai Annie. "Nobody say anything. I call lawyer from station."

"But there's only ninety minutes left before—" Max said.

"I know," said Annie. "I know."

Following a short ride across the river, the S.P.I.E.S. team was marched into a brown-and-tan brick office building that seemed more like the home of an engineering firm than a police station. Nevertheless, it still possessed that unique smell of burned coffee, flop sweat, and lies that marks police stations the world over.

The duty officer at the front desk (Sergeant Yee, by his nameplate) separated the adults from the teens, calmly ignoring Hantai Annie Wong's strenuous protests. As the constables hauled off Annie, Stones, and Simon, Max's father called, "Don't worry, son. We'll get you out of here."

Max lifted a hand in farewell at the sight of his father disappearing down the corridor. An unexpected pang gripped his heart. In all the brief time they had spent together, there had been far too many good-byes.

"Now, let's get you tykes sorted out," said Sergeant Yee, an amiable Asian man tall enough to be a first-string basketball player. "We'll need to contact your legal guardians."

"Those *are* our legal guardians," Max and Cinnabar chimed in together.

"Oh," said the sergeant. He blinked. "Well, er, we'll make sure they're present when you're questioned. Now off with you."

Hard-faced cops escorted the five teens to an isolated holding cell with six crummy-looking cots and a toilet, clanging the door shut on them. The key turned, the constables left, and the junior spies were alone with their thoughts.

Not very pleasant thoughts, to be sure.

Max slumped onto the cot and sank his head in his hands. This was it. Once the police learned that Merry Sunshine Orphanage didn't actually have a home anymore, they'd split up Max and his friends and hand them over to social workers for placement with foster parents. Max too, since his father had been part of the group breaking into Parliament.

Or—worst case—now that they were all lawbreakers, the cops might dump the teens into juvenile hall.

And it was all his fault.

Max's stomach churned. He'd been too greedy. He'd wanted everything—a father *and* his orphanage friends *and* a career as a spy. This cell, this was where greediness led. He should have known that orphans don't get happy endings.

"Fool," he muttered.

"I couldn't agree more," said Nikki.

Max couldn't even bring himself to trade insults with her.

His forehead resting against the bars, Wyatt stared at a scuffed patch of concrete floor. "I saw on TV that if they arrest you under the Terrorist Act, they can hold you for up to fourteen days before even charging you."

"*Now* who's a ray of sunshine?" said Cinnabar.

Wyatt lifted a shoulder. "I'm just saying. . . ."

"We need to do something more productive here."

Nikki sneered. "What, like carve our names into the wall?"

"No," said Cinnabar. "Like figure out where LOTUS will make their move."

"What's the point?" muttered Max, not lifting his eyes.

"The point," said Cinnabar, her voice sharpening, "is that we're the only ones who can stop them. It's all up to us."

Nikki snorted. "Then this country's in big trouble."

"Enough, Nikki!" snapped Tremaine, coming to his feet. "She's right—we've gotta do *something*."

"Hey, guys?" said Wyatt.

The redheaded girl lunged to standing, face flushed. "Don't act all boss man with me, Natty Dread. I happen to agree with her. It's only that we're, you know, *in jail*."

"Guys?" Wyatt tried again.

Tremaine's eyes narrowed to dangerous slits. *"Natty Dread?* You did *not* just call me Natty Dread. You think, 'cause I'm from Jamaica, that—"

"Oi!" yelled Wyatt. "Shut it!" The two of them broke off squabbling, and Wyatt blinked in surprise at his own shout. "Look, I think we're going about this the wrong way."

"How do you mean?" asked Cinnabar.

Wyatt ran his fingers through his unruly blond curls, scrubbing at his scalp as if to stimulate his thinking. "Well, we all assumed that, because LOTUS is after government ministers, they'd strike at the Houses of Parliament."

Sunk deep in his own misery, Max had mostly let the conversation wash over him. But at this, he raised his head. "But . . . Parliament's one of the most heavily guarded spots in the country."

"Exactly," said Wyatt. He spread his hands. "Too much security. So what if LOTUS was never planning to meet there at all?"

"You mean . . . ?" Cinnabar said.

"What if they want the ministers to come to *them*?"

Nikki frowned, drawn into it despite herself. "But how? What does a bleeding minister like?"

"A party?" said Tremaine.

"A fund-raiser?" said Max.

Cinnabar's mouth fell open and her golden eyes widened. "A circus."

Everyone regarded her strangely. "Say what?" said Nikki.

"I saw an invitation in that MP's office," said Cinnabar. "Cirque du . . . Something."

Max jolted upright, galvanized. "Chat. Cirque du Chat— there was a poster in Mrs. Frost's office. And *chat* means—"

" 'Cat,' in French," said Nikki. Now everyone stared at *her* strangely. "What? I've been to school, you know. Plonkers."

Wyatt snapped his fingers. "Of course!" he cried. "That smell when we were leaving LOTUS HQ. It's not just the one tiger; it's the stink of the big cats' cages. She must have a bunch of 'em."

Tremaine raised an eyebrow. "Uh, and you know this how?"

"My gran worked in the circus," said Wyatt. "They used to call me—"

"The Cat Whisperer," said Max and Cinnabar together. "We know."

Stroking his chin, Wyatt said, "But performing circuses are banned here. . . . LOTUS must have gotten some kind of special dispensation. I wonder—"

"Brilliant," said Nikki, with sarcasm thick enough to frost a wedding cake. "So you're Little Joey Cat Boy, and LOTUS is gonna brainwash all those pols in a circus tonight. How does that help? As I pointed out earlier, we're in jail."

Tremaine gripped the bars, gazing up at the surveillance camera in a corner of the room. "We could tell them. If only the cops knew that we broke into Parliament for good reason. We could explain—"

"Waste of time." Nikki snorted. "You think they'd care? All the fuzz care about is the law, and we broke it."

"True enough," said Cinnabar. "Then I guess that means we'll have to bust out."

A long pause followed that remark. Tremaine smiled.

"Of here?" said Nikki. "Have you gone completely barking mad? I like breaking laws as much as the next girl, but that'd only land us in worse trouble than we're in already."

Cinnabar bristled. "I don't hear you coming up with any better ideas."

The bigger girl growled and stared down at Cinn. But she didn't say anything. She truly didn't have any better ideas.

Max shifted back and forth. A fragile sense of hope made his limbs tingle. There *had* to be a way out. If he could only think . . .

"Did anyone manage to keep their lock picks?" asked Tremaine.

Nobody had.

"Any smoke bombs or flash grenades or experimental bang-bang chewing gum?" asked Wyatt.

None.

Cinnabar paced the confines of their cell, scanning high and low. Max could've saved her the trouble. The windows bristled with steel bars, and the only drain was about six inches across. No great escapes happening there.

"We could try a . . . diversion," she said. "Start a fight or something, and when the cops rush in, we knock them out and escape."

This time Tremaine shook his head. "Cho! This isn't the movies, sister. These blokes have seen those tricks before."

"Well, we can't just sit around waiting for our fairy god-mother while LOTUS brainwashes half the government." Cinnabar threw up her hands. "Think!"

Max raised a finger. "Fairy godmother?"

"Too bad you don't have one, Maxi-Pad," Nikki sneered. "She could get you a date and cure your zits, both."

A faint smile hovered around his lips. "Oh, but I do," he said. "And aren't we allowed one phone call?"

One phone call, some extravagant promises, and an excruciating wait later, the fairy godmother arrived. And unlike most folktales, he arrived in the person of an eccentric billionaire named Reginald Demetrius Elbow.

"This had better not be some kind of trick," sniffed Mr. Elbow, standing outside their cell with a small army of lawyers and a pair of bodyguards straight out of a wrestling promoter's dream. With his liquid brown eyes, goatee, and chiseled cheekbones, the billionaire resembled a Chinese Johnny Depp. If you squinted.

"No trick," said Max. "You get us out of here, and we get you back the mind-control device."

Max didn't bother mentioning that there were a few ifs involved. *If* Hantai Annie would agree to this deal he'd just made on S.P.I.E.S.'s behalf. *If* they could actually arrive in time to stop LOTUS. And *if* the cops didn't impound the device afterward for evidence.

All these ifs were need-to-know only, and he figured that right now Mr. Elbow didn't really need to know.

With a wave of their fairy godfather's magic wand (and some Rottweiler-aggressive legal work), soon they were all— adults included—standing on the sidewalk outside the police station. Max didn't ask how. All he knew was, it paid to know eccentric billionaires with friends in high places.

"*Yoku yatta*, Max-*kun*," said Hantai Annie. "Well done."

Simon Segredo clapped his son on the shoulder and left his hand there. Max didn't shrug it off.

"Genius move," said Max's father. "You're a chip off the old block—off both old blocks. Your mum would be proud."

At the praise, Max felt his face grow warm.

"Now remember, Mrs. Wong, the lot of you are on probation," said Sergeant Yee, standing on the steps above them. "One misstep, one illegal activity, and *ffwit!*—back in the clink you go."

"You can be certain, Sergeant," said Mr. Elbow, "that if she and her team do not fulfill their promises, Mr. Elbow will lock their cell door himself."

The tall sergeant stepped down and extended his hand. "Mr. Elbow, sir, it's been a real honor."

The billionaire stared at the proffered palm as if it were a tarantula-and-rattlesnake sandwich.

"Mr. Elbow don't shake," said one of the bodyguards.

"Right, then," said Sergeant Yee. He executed a flawless salute. "A real honor," he repeated, then pivoted and marched back into the building.

The billionaire let his imperious stare roam over the S.P.I.E.S. team, stopping at Hantai Annie. "Well? Where's my device?"

"First," said the spymaster, "we must learn location of circus."

"Is that all?" Mr. Elbow snapped his fingers, demanding his cell phone. In a few moments, he'd reached someone. "Jack? It's Mr. Elbow. Fine, thanks. Listen, where's that cat circus happening tonight? Right, right. Ta, Jack. Best to the missus."

"Who's Jack?" Max whispered to his father.

"The prime minister," said the billionaire, overhearing him. He turned to Hantai Annie and told her the name of the park where the circus was being held.

Simon rubbed his jaw. "But that's easily a half hour away by car, and the show starts in fifteen minutes."

Mr. Elbow smiled a patronizing smile. And just like that, the air filled with the *whup-whup-whup* of a large passenger helicopter, which whirred over a nearby building and landed smack in the center of the traffic roundabout. Drivers swerved, honked, and swore.

"You were saying?" said the billionaire. He strode toward the chopper, bodyguards in tow.

"Wow," murmured Wyatt. "I wonder if he wants to adopt any orphans?"

CHAPTER 25

THE LIONS' LEAP

SEEN FROM ABOVE, the park was a diamond of darkness adrift in a sea of city lights. The helicopter's spotlight picked out stretches of trees and lawn, the sudden sparkle of a small rowing lake.

But the spotlight was unnecessary. At one end of the park, lit up like the prime pastry in a bakeshop window was an enormous red-and-yellow tent.

The big top.

The pilot landed his chopper on a vacant stretch of lawn, and as the S.P.I.E.S. crew disembarked, two really fit women with gear bags came trotting up, courtesy of Mr. Elbow. One woman passed Max his jet pack, which he greeted with a cry of "Come to Papa!"

Cinnabar peered around Mr. Stones's shoulder as he unzipped one of the bags. It held smoke bombs, a variety of tools, and a pair of very serious-looking pistols.

254

"Lookie lookie, cupcake," Stones shouted over the roar of the rotors. "Just what the doctor ordered."

Giving the group a thumbs-up, Mr. Elbow leaned back in his seat with a cold beverage. Clearly, he planned on getting nowhere near the action.

Everyone crowded around for their equipment, and Hantai Annie had to take one of the pistols away from Nikki. Cinnabar blew out a sigh of relief. Nikki and firearms was a seriously bad combination.

The spymaster led her little group away to the cover of some trees, where they could hear one another better. She gestured at them to form a huddle.

"*Minna, yoku kike*," said Annie. "Listen up. This is our most important mission ever."

Cinnabar felt a little shiver dance along her spine. And she didn't think it was due to the chilly wind off the lake.

"LOTUS has more resources," said the spymaster. "More manpower. Odds are against us, but we have one big advantage."

"Surprise?" guessed Max.

Hantai Annie held a fist to her heart. "Goodness. No matter what we face, we fight for justice."

"Yer bloody well right," said Stones, eyeing the circle of faces with a half-crazed grin. "And there's no one I'd rather face impossible odds with than this bunch of plonkers."

Simon Segredo nodded. "I've only been with you all a short while, but you've taught me so much about family."

"That it can be a real pain in the bum?" said Wyatt, to laughter.

"And a true inspiration," said Mr. Segredo. "It's an honor to take on this mission with you." At that, Max beamed.

A warm rush spread through Cinnabar's chest. She squeezed Max's shoulder on one side, Wyatt's on the other. These (and her sister, Jazz, of course) were her family, her people. With them, she could face anything.

"How do we do this?" she asked.

Hantai Annie guided them closer to the big top. At this distance, it glowed like a huge Japanese lantern, trailing long strings of lights to the ground on every side. The lights also served to illuminate a number of agents in dark suits or silver-and-black spandex, standing at regular intervals around the perimeter.

"They are night-blind," whispered the spymaster. "Too close to lights."

"What a shame," said Mr. Segredo, with a rakish grin. "Then they won't know what hit them."

Annie gave instructions, dividing her crew into three teams—Tremaine and Nikki for distraction, and the rest split into two units that would infiltrate the tent from either side.

"But how do we get in?" Wyatt asked.

Mr. Stones slid a razor-edged knife from its sheath and whipped it around like a ninja. "Don't worry, sunshine," he said. "Love will find a way."

A roar went up from inside the tent. A flourish of trumpets.

The show had begun.

Cinnabar took her position behind some bushes, beyond the nimbus of light cast by the tent. With her waited Mr. Segredo and Max. At the signal, Tremaine bopped along the lit pathway to the big top, earbuds in place, as if he were rocking out to his own private sound track.

Two beefy LOTUS agents left their posts by the entrance and swaggered toward him. Just before they arrived, Tremaine whipped out a flashbang and tossed it at their feet, simultaneously leaping aside.

Foomf! The explosion rocked the spies, tossing them backward onto the lawn like discarded dolls, temporarily blinded and deafened. The concussion overlapped with another roar from the crowd in the tent.

Cinnabar chewed her lip. What was happening inside? Would they make it in time?

Spotting the flashbang explosion, the nearest LOTUS agent spoke some quick words into her sleeve and hustled forward, weapon at the ready.

Pow! From out of the darkness, the blast of Nikki's paintball gun took the agent down—not with paint, but with a concentrated ball of pepper-spray gunk. As two more spies rounded the far corner of the big top, Tremaine lobbed a teargas grenade. Then he and Nikki faded back into the trees, luring the other LOTUS agents away.

"Now!" said Mr. Segredo.

He, Max, and Cinnabar ran full speed for the tent. With

his long blade, Mr. Segredo hacked a V in the canvas, and he and Max dove through it, tucking and rolling to their feet in unison. Cinnabar plunged after them, into a bewildering world of noise and lights and smells. Popcorn, hay, and that funky cat stink from LOTUS HQ assaulted Cinnabar's nose. She blinked, eyes adjusting to the brightness.

The trio found themselves behind rows of theater seats mounted on bleachers. Although she couldn't see the action in the center of the big top, Cinnabar noticed the myriad of twinkling fairy lights, the multicolored lasers arcing back and forth, and the red-and-yellow tint cast upon all the people inside.

Some kind of strange circus-y hip-hop blared through the speakers, only to be overpowered by an amplified voice.

"Thank you, ladies and gentlemen, honored ministers," said Mrs. Frost from some unseen location. "But that is merely a taste of what's to come. Behold, the Lions' Leap!"

The crack of a whip. The blast of trumpets.

Cinnabar, Max, and his father crept into an aisle between bleacher sections, and now they could see what fascinated the audience of posh men and women, power brokers all.

The broad center ring was surrounded by what must have been more than twenty big cats. On individual golden stands, lions, tigers, leopards, and black panthers sat obediently, eyes glowing in the reddish light like hot coals. Seven women in black-and-silver spandex wheeled in an odd metal structure with a number of platforms set in a circle.

Another whipcrack, and a shouted command from the ringmaster, a diminutive figure in top hat, red tailcoat, and black boots. She half turned, and Cinnabar recognized the grandmotherly woman.

"Frost," hissed Mr. Segredo. "She always did like to crack the whip."

At Mrs. Frost's command, two lions, a tiger, and a leopard left their stands and slunk forward, climbing onto the platforms in the center ring. Cinnabar sucked in her breath, awed by the graceful strength of their movements. As often as you see big cats on TV, she thought, you never get just how powerful and truly *big* they are.

Mrs. Frost gestured to her helpers, and now the platforms began to raise the four predators into the air as the structure revealed its nature. It was an irregular series of circular stands, with long vertical gaps between them, and it extended from the ground to the very top of the tent, at least a hundred feet above.

When the lifts stopped, the big cats poked their heads over the edge and snarled at the crowd far below.

"They're going to jump to those little stands?" said Max. "One miss, and splat goes the cat."

"Watch for the mind-control device," said Mr. Segredo. "All this circus stuff is merely a distraction."

"Oh, right," said Cinnabar, who'd gotten completely caught up in the pageantry. She lowered her gaze to find that several LOTUS agents had discovered their presence and were sprinting down the aisle. "Look out!" she cried.

"I'll hold them off," said Max's father.

The two forward agents skipped, turned their skips into front handsprings, and came flipping toward Mr. Segredo like a pair of evil acrobats. He pulled something from his pouch that resembled a mass of cord with three black rubber balls attached, whirled it once, twice, three times around his head, and let go.

Spinning through the air, the contraption wrapped around the lead spy's face like an attack octopus. The balls struck him several sharp blows. He collapsed, and with a few punches and kicks, Mr. Segredo made short work of the second acrobat.

From behind the downed agents, Ebelskeever loomed, roaring, "I've got you, Segredo!"

"You most certainly do," said Max's father. He clenched his fists and waded into battle with a savage grin.

Max caught Cinnabar's arm. "Come on!" he cried, dodging back behind the bleachers. "Let's find the invention."

They raced around the perimeter, eyes peeled for other LOTUS agents and the distinctive blue cube of the mind-control device.

"You know what I've been wondering?" Cinnabar half shouted over the crowd's oohs and aahs.

"What?" said Max.

"How she's going to brainwash all these people. I mean, that headset only fits over one head at a time, right?"

"Right."

"So, are they brainwashing the ministers one by one while everyone's distracted, or what?" she asked.

Max's perplexed expression changed to one of alarm as he spotted something. "Watch out!"

He grabbed the support pole on the rear corner of the bleachers, kicked off, and swung his body around horizontally. *Whump!* His feet struck a spandex-clad LOTUS agent squarely in the chest. The spy stumbled backward across the aisle, smacking his head on the next set of bleachers.

As he sagged to the ground, Cinnabar rushed forward and zapped him with her Taser. The man twitched and lay still, out cold.

Retrieving the jet pack that had fallen off during his attack, Max slipped his arms back into the straps.

"Really?" said Cinnabar. "After all the trouble it's given you, you still want to use that?"

One side of his mouth turned up in a smirk. "A spy's gotta have his gadgets."

Cinnabar couldn't argue with that. Boys and their toys.

A deafening round of applause signaled the end of the Lions' Leap performance. Cinnabar felt almost disappointed that she'd missed it. After all, an orphan girl didn't get out to the circus that often. (Try never.)

But she and Max had more than enough to occupy their attention. Down the next corridor they passed, Cinnabar glimpsed the center ring. The predators had returned to their regular platforms, and Mrs. Frost stood beside the tall structure holding something new. Something familiar.

"There it is!" cried Cinnabar, clutching Max's sleeve.

And sure enough, the ringmaster now grasped the cobalt-blue cube of the mind-control device in one hand. With the other, she brought the microphone to her lips. "And now, for our final act, the one I like to call . . . the Big Payback. Because when you damage one's livelihood and deny her the honors she deserves, there is always *payback*." Even from this distance, her storm-gray eyes were eerie and electric.

The audience murmured in confusion as Mrs. Frost set down her mike and adjusted the dials. Cinnabar got a queasy feeling in the pit of her stomach.

"What's she up to?" said Max.

"I don't know," said Cinnabar, "but we've got to stop it."

They sped down the aisle, heading for the center ring. On the opposite side, Cinnabar spied Hantai Annie Wong and Wyatt running to help. But they would all be too late.

Mrs. Frost pressed one last button, and spoke two simple words.

"Ready . . ."

All at once, the lions, tigers, leopards, and panthers shifted on their platforms to face the audience.

"*Killll!*" shrieked the evil ringmaster.

And the big cats pounced.

THE CAT WHISPERER

UTTER PANDEMONIUM. The government ministers screamed and scrambled up the bleachers, trying to escape the onrushing predators. Men trampled women; women shoved men. Dignity forgotten, every audience member at once attempted to go up or out. But steel bars now blocked the entrances, and the bleachers only stretched so high.

Nowhere in that tent was safe.

And through it all, the creepy hip-hop circus tune kept grinding on.

As he sprinted toward the center ring, Wyatt gaped at the insane simplicity of Mrs. Frost's plan. She didn't want to control the government, she wanted to destroy it. And she hadn't brainwashed the ministers.

She'd brainwashed the big cats. Somehow LOTUS had modified the device to work on all of them.

Wyatt screwed up his face. A surge of pity swelled in his heart for those magnificent animals.

Ahead of him, Hantai Annie dashed into the center ring, intending to snatch the blue cube, but Mrs. Frost saw her coming. The LOTUS chief lashed her whip to drive Annie back, and then hopped onto a platform, tossing the weapon aside. With the flip of a switch, her stand began to rise.

"You can't stop them, not even with the device," the ringmaster cried. "Only I can—*unh!*"

Hantai Annie had taken a kung fu leap, catching the edge of the platform with one arm and Mrs. Frost's ankle with the other. The older woman toppled, but managed to keep both the invention and her place on the stand.

She kicked savagely at Annie's face, still rising.

Hearing a fresh round of screams in the bleachers, Wyatt tore his eyes away from the fight. Maybe he couldn't help his spymaster. But he could help all those doomed ministers.

His eye fell on the microphone, lying abandoned on the sawdust in the center ring. In three long strides, he grasped it.

"Rrroar," he said into the mike. *Wow.* His amplified voice sounded so loud, so weird, that Wyatt immediately choked up in embarrassment. He shrank. Who was he to be the loudest person, the tallest poppy, the voice of authority?

"Help! Somebody help!" cried a tall, regal-looking woman. A white tiger had caught a corner of her long evening gown in its jaws, and she was whacking at the creature with her purse. Wyatt knew, as soon as the tiger finished playing with her, it would gobble the woman up.

Somebody had to do something. And that somebody, like it or not, was him.

Wyatt sucked in a deep breath. "ROOOAAARRR!" he called with more authority. A few of the lions slowed their stalking approach, twitching their ears and peering about for the source of the sound.

"Chuff chuff chuff . . ." he crooned, switching to the tone that had earned him the title of Cat Whisperer, all those years ago at Gran's circus. He closed his eyes, shutting out the pandemonium and the fear, pouring all his focus into those soothing sounds. With the familiar smell of sawdust, hay, and big cat in his nostrils, Wyatt could almost believe he was back in his gran's care, safe and loved and cherished.

With family.

"Kimmm-murmur-murmur . . ."

Into his wordless song, he poured all those feelings of loving and belonging, all his desire to return to those simpler times, when he was just a little kid and everything was all right. Wyatt didn't know how long he kept up the crooning. It could've been a minute, it could've been a day.

When he came back to himself, the first thing he noticed was a strong odor of raw meat and cat food. Wyatt opened his eyes.

He stood at the center point of twenty-something pairs

of yellow eyes, gazing raptly up at him. He was completely surrounded by a small ocean of fur and fang and muscle. By the biggest of the big cats.

Wyatt swallowed. "Nice kitties?" he said.

As Hantai Annie jumped for the rising platform, Max and Cinnabar charged down the aisle to help. All at once, a towering figure blocked their way.

"Not so fast," snarled Styx, the massive double agent. "You've both got a lot to answer for." He held no weapon, but then he didn't need one—his powerful hands were the size of dinner plates. Styx spread his arms wide, barring the path.

They couldn't slip past him, and the bleachers were crawling with panicked politicians—no way through up there either.

With a sinking feeling, Max regretted pepper-spraying the thick man.

"I suppose it's too late to kiss and make up?" he said.

Styx pounded his huge fist into his palm. His smile was an ugly thing to behold. "Normally, I don't approve of violence against kids, but—"

"Don't go making an exception for us," said Cinnabar. Her tone was light, but Max noticed the tightness in her voice and the set of her shoulders.

The spy lumbered forward, snatching at them like a giant from a fairy tale. Max and Cinnabar danced backward out

of reach. Once more, he grabbed and they evaded. Styx was forcing them away from the center ring.

Past the big man's shoulder, Max saw the platform lift as Mrs. Frost kicked at Hantai Annie. The younger woman avoided Frost's attack, but lost her grip on the stand, and tumbled into thin air.

"No!"

Instinctively, Max curled his arms above his head as if to protect himself. His chest felt tight. He couldn't lose Hantai Annie—he just couldn't.

"Styx," pleaded Cinnabar. "Let us go. Annie could die."

"Tough toenails," growled the double agent, rubbing the bruise on his temple. "Let her."

The platforms continued to rise, and now Max saw that Hantai Annie had landed on a lower one, and was dangling off it, half-dazed. Frost was climbing to her feet.

"Go!" said Cinnabar, drawing a wide-barreled weapon from her waistband.

"But I can't—" Max gestured at the angry agent closing in on them.

She rolled her eyes. "Fly, you cabbage brain!"

Duh. Max had nearly forgotten about his jet pack. He reached for the starter button as Cinnabar fired three bean-bag rounds—*bam-bam-bam*—into Styx's broad chest.

"Unh!" The big man staggered back a step, barely fazed. Cinnabar fumbled in her pockets for a reload.

Max hesitated, torn between helping Cinnabar and helping Annie.

Then Styx gave an animal bellow of pain and dropped to one knee. Behind him stood Cinnabar's sister, Jazz, dressed all in black and recovering from the kick she'd just delivered. "Get away from my sister," she snarled.

"Jazz!" cried Cinnabar.

A grinning Mr. Stones stepped up beside Jazz, hefting a lead-filled blackjack in one hand.

"Aww, does widdle Styxie have a sore knee?" he said. Stones winked at Max. "Go ahead, cupcake. We got this one."

Max didn't need to hear it twice. He yanked at the joystick and zoomed straight up. One of Styx's huge hands rose to snatch him out of the air, but Cinnabar, Jazz, and Stones closed on the traitor, taking him down.

Then Max was past them, soaring up into the lights, homing in on Hantai Annie. Movement from above caught his eye. Max saw Mrs. Frost draw something from inside her jacket, something that glinted in the spotlight.

A pistol.

She would shoot Hantai Annie before the spymaster could recover! Max was closing on them, but he wouldn't make it in time. *No!* Desperate, he pawed at his pockets for something to throw, and came up with one of the smoke bombs.

With his hands off the controls, the jet pack wobbled in its flight like a nectar-crazed hummingbird, and Max nearly slipped out of his harness. Awkwardly, he heaved the bomb at Mrs. Frost from about a dozen feet away.

It struck the ringmaster a glancing blow on the cheek, knocking her off balance, but not off the platform. Max steadied his flight, but he was fresh out of weapons.

And now Mrs. Frost was aiming the pistol at *him*!

Yikes.

"Witless, brainless boy!" she shrieked. *"No one* stops my revenge!"

He yanked the joystick forward, zooming lower around the structure's central cylinder, just as a bullet pinged off the steel core above his head.

"No!" cried Annie.

Max held his jet pack to a tight arc, hugging the frame with a skill he didn't know he possessed.

As he came around again, Max noticed Mrs. Frost's forgotten whip, dangling off a lower platform. He reached out an arm and snagged it, jerking back on the joystick to rise again.

Just ahead, he saw a sight that chilled him to the marrow: Hantai Annie crouching on her platform like a fox cornered by hunters on a high cliff. And above her, Mrs. Frost. The ringmaster leaned over the edge, steadying her pistol in a two-handed grip.

At that range, she couldn't miss.

"Any last words?" Mrs. Frost called, her voice all ice and steel.

"*Nanakorobi yaoki*," said Hantai Annie, her eyes never leaving her enemy.

The LOTUS chief sneered. "In English?"

Hantai Annie Wong squared her shoulders, body as full of tension as a coiled spring. "Fall seven times, stand up eight," she said.

"Not this time," said Mrs. Frost, drawing a bead on Annie.

Max had only one chance to get this right. As he zoomed toward them, he swung his arm back, pulling the whip with it, then lashed forward with all his might.

Whh-chack! The leather popper at the whip's end tore into the soft skin of Mrs. Frost's hands. With a cry, she released the pistol. It tumbled into Hantai Annie's waiting grip.

"Ha!" Max crowed. "Take that!"

But he was robbed of seeing Mrs. Frost's reaction, because when Max snapped the whip, he'd lost command of the jet pack. *No, not again.* For a handful of heart-stopping seconds, he whizzed about like a balloon releasing its air, legs swinging, nearly cracking his head on a platform above him.

His ragged breath burst in and out. A crash from this height could kill him.

Max gritted his teeth. He wasn't going to crash—not this time.

With a Herculean effort, he righted himself and leveled off. Max took the jet pack in a wide circuit through the smoky, laser-lit air, coming around to hover beside Hantai Annie's platform.

She glanced over at him, keeping the weapon trained on Mrs. Frost. "Not bad, Max-*kun*, not bad. We may make a spy of you yet."

. . . AND THROW AWAY THE KEY

BY THE TIME the police, zookeepers, and MI5 arrived, summoned by a quick-thinking minister, things were settling down in the big top. Somehow or other, Wyatt truly *was* a cat whisperer, and had guided the predators safely back into their cages, to the everlasting amazement of the zookeepers. He stayed beside the big cats, feeding the creatures morsels of raw meat and murmuring to them in his daft way.

Once the cats had been corralled, the politicians climbed down from their bleachers and started behaving like politicians again, instead of frightened nanny goats. That meant lots of bluster and bravado and ordering people about. Business as usual. While a few ministers had been pawed, nobody had been seriously injured, much less eaten.

Cinnabar felt bad for the disappointed cats, but she supposed that, on the whole, it was rather a good thing.

For all their size and strength, Styx and Ebelskeever hadn't prevailed either. A battered Ebelskeever sat handcuffed in the back of a police van, while the half-conscious Styx was being watched over and occasionally tormented by the gleefully revengeful Stones.

And speaking of vengeance, Cinnabar briefly came face-to-face with Vespa da Costa in the crowd. Her stomach hardened and an involuntary tigerlike growl rumbled from her throat.

But when she noticed how lost and distressed the blond girl seemed, Cinnabar resisted the urge to punch her right in her frog-lipped mouth.

"Cinnabar!" Vespa cried, reaching out as if for support, then letting her hand fall. "I . . . are you okay?"

"Yes, no thanks to you," snapped Cinnabar.

"Me?" Vespa's brown eyes went wide. "But I had nothing to do with all this."

"I'll bet."

"It's true. In fact, I'm the one who brought your sister here."

"Right." Cinnabar folded her arms. "You brought Jazz here."

"It's true, sis," said Jazz, materializing from the crowd. "She wanted to help."

Jazz seemed sincere, but Cinnabar wasn't ready to let Vespa off the hook so easily. "So how did you *know* to bring her here?" she demanded. "You must have been in on the plot."

"I guessed something was going to happen, but I didn't know what." The blond girl held up her palms. "I swear. It's all my aunt's doing."

"Oh, really." Cinnabar cocked her head.

"She forced me to come to this," said Vespa. "I didn't know what she had planned. She said I had some growing up to do, and that I should watch and learn."

"And did you?" asked Jazz gently.

Vespa's head drooped, and her soft hair fell like a curtain. For a second, jealousy of the girl's perfect, tangle-free golden locks wrestled with compassion in Cinnabar's heart.

"I learned that just because someone is your blood relative, that doesn't make them a good person," she said.

"Or even sane," said Cinnabar.

Vespa nodded. "That too. Blood isn't everything. But family . . ." Her eyes grew moist. "I wish I had a family like you two, and Wyatt, and Max."

At the mention of his name, Cinnabar's eyes narrowed. "You keep your paws off Max."

The blond girl raised her palms again in surrender and wandered off into the crowd. Jazz laughed and lightly punched her sister's shoulder. "Possessive much?" she said.

Cinnabar blushed and looked away. Near the entrance, she noticed Mrs. Frost in handcuffs, surrounded by police, and she wondered what would become of Vespa, what would become of them all.

S.P.I.E.S. had done it. They had defeated LOTUS, at least in this country. But was this their swan song? Without a home, without resources, could the Merry Sunshine orphans stay together?

Max joined his father near the entrance, where Simon and Hantai Annie Wong stood talking with several important-looking politicians in expensive suits. His father flashed him a quick smile and draped his arm, warm and heavy, around Max's shoulder. Somehow, it just felt right.

". . . and with half of Parliament to testify," a lean, caramel-skinned woman was saying, "I rather doubt we'll have much trouble locking these villains up."

Hantai Annie's lips tightened. "You don't know them, Khambaita-*san*. Mrs. Frost has resources, high-placed connections. She is—*∂ou üu ka?*—slippery like eel."

"Deputy Director," said Simon to the woman, "I have something that may be of use in building a substantial case against them."

"Oh?"

He fished a thumb drive from his pocket and passed it over. "Evidence," he said. "Evidence of terrorist acts, both here and abroad."

The deputy director handed the storage device to an

assistant, who produced a compact laptop computer and plugged it in. After clicking and scrolling through one or two files, he wore a smile wide enough to drive a train through.

"Well?" said Mrs. Khambaita.

"We're good," said the assistant. "Tip-top, in fact. What a pleasure it will be to lock them up and melt down the key."

Deputy Director Khambaita inclined her head toward Max's father. "You have the thanks of MI5," she said, "both of you." Now she included Hantai Annie. "I'm not sure where our government would be without you."

"In a tiger's belly?" said Max.

Annie scowled at his impudence, but Max's father smothered a smile and squeezed his shoulder.

"Er, yes," said Mrs. Khambaita. "Precisely." She rounded up her entourage and started to leave, but then wheeled back to say, "Your government won't forget this, Mrs. Wong. Truly."

Hantai Annie gave a gruff nod. When the important-looking people had moved out of earshot, she muttered, "Government promises. Hmph!"

But the glitter in her dark eyes told Max she was pleased with how things had transpired. Just then, he spotted Wyatt by the big cat cages, and said, "Back in a flash." Breaking away, he threaded through overturned chairs and small knots of shaken politicians.

Over by the cages, the musky scent of the huge felines

was enough to make your eyes water. But Wyatt didn't seem to notice. He sat on a bale of hay, humming a little tune and occasionally tossing chunks of meat from a bowl into the nearest cages. The predators watched with what Max would've sworn was something like adoration.

"Cat whisperer, eh?" he said, sitting next to Wyatt.

The blond boy shrugged a shoulder and cleared his throat. "Something like that."

"That was amazing," said Max.

"You saw?"

"A little," Max admitted. "In between flying around and getting shot at. You're a real hero."

Wyatt blushed. "Nah . . ."

Max bumped his shoulder. "Really, truly," he said. "You're not a sidekick or tech support like you say. You're the real deal."

The blond boy swallowed hard, glancing away. He cleared his throat again and let his gaze roam around the big top. "What a night," he said.

"What a night."

Shaking his head, Wyatt continued, "Who would've thought, when we first saw that mind-control device, that this is what Mrs. Frost intended."

"Yeah," said Max. "What a raving loon—" He stopped dead, struck by a thought.

"What?" asked Wyatt.

"Where is it?"

Wyatt frowned. "The invention? Dunno, mate. I sort of lost track of it."

A tingling began in Max's chest, and he shot to his feet. Where *was* it? Had some LOTUS agent managed to spirit away the device, despite the best efforts of the police?

"Max?" said Wyatt.

But Max was up and running toward the center ring. The motor controlling the Lions' Leap structure had jammed after the police arrived, and the constables had used ladders to bring down Mrs. Frost and Hantai Annie. Was the mind-control device still on the platform?

Powering up the jet pack, Max rose into the air, his breath coming short and fast. At last, his eyes cleared the level of Mrs. Frost's stand—and there it was, the blue cube that had caused all this trouble. Well, maybe not *all* the trouble, Max amended. LOTUS had had plenty to do with it as well.

He reached out his hands, lifted the invention, and pulled it close. Then he very carefully sank to a landing in the center ring. Only when his feet were on the ground did Max let out a gusty sigh of relief.

"Mr. Elbow will take that, thanks awfully," said a familiar voice. At his side stood the billionaire, eyes shining and hands outstretched.

For a few heartbeats, Max hesitated. This was an incredibly dangerous and powerful invention. Why should he hand it over to this bizarre man, who might use it for even worse purposes than LOTUS?

Because they'd struck a deal, that's why. And because Mr. Elbow, odd as he was, had helped them defeat Frost and LOTUS.

"Here," Max said, passing over the cube. It didn't seem quite right, but after the exhausting day he'd had, he couldn't think of what else to do.

Mr. Elbow cradled the mind-control device like a baby, and Max was reminded of that creepy bloke in *The Lord of the Rings* who totally obsessed over the ring.

"Do we get some kind of reward?" Max asked, thinking of Merry Sunshine's troubled finances.

"Reward?" The billionaire didn't take his eyes off the cube. "You're alive and free and British—that should be reward enough." Still gazing at his prized possession, Mr. Elbow headed for the entrance, relying on his bodyguards to clear a path.

That's all very well for you, thought Max, but what about us?

NORMAL IS OVERRATED

CHAPTER 28

THE FOLLOWING WEEK, he found out.

Reunited at last, the entire S.P.I.E.S. crew had been staying in temporary quarters, a disused dormitory for the criminally insane. (Nikki had made plenty of jokes at Max's expense over that—though he'd pointed out that *she* was living there too.)

Mr. Vazquez showed up with a still-healing Rashid, fresh from hospital. Even Max's dad was staying with them. His dad. After all their complicated history, Max found that he finally thought of Simon that way—as Dad—although he wasn't quite used to calling him that yet.

One morning, Hantai Annie received a phone call, very hush-hush. She told none of the orphans what was said, only that they had a lunchtime appointment, and that everyone should get ready.

At the arranged time, the whole crew piled into several gleaming Mercedes SUVs. Max watched out the window as they wound their way deeper into the capital, and then veered into one of the more exclusive districts of posh homes.

His brow furrowed. "Where are we going?"

"You'll see," was all the spymaster would say.

Streets began to seem more and more familiar. Finally, they turned up a road Max knew quite well.

"But, LOTUS HQ is on this street," said Wyatt.

"Sou ∂a," said the spymaster mildly.

And then, their van pulled into the driveway of the sprawling mansion they had rescued Max from only a week before.

"Um, where are we going?" said Cinnabar.

"You know where," said Hantai Annie.

"But why?" said Max.

She offered only a sphinxlike smile in reply.

After parking on the familiar gravel patch, Hantai Annie Wong led her charges inside. As they passed through the spotless entryway, Max couldn't repress a shudder at the thought of his time here, at the thought that he nearly became a permanent resident.

And now they were just walking in of their own free will?

"Hello, sports fans!" called a cheerful voice. It was Vespa, but what a changed Vespa. She wore a tailored silk pantsuit, her hair shone like the sun, and her smile was as broad and carefree as a beach in Brazil.

"Um, hi?" Max choked out. Suddenly he felt all warm and funny. Vespa really was a knockout.

Cinnabar scowled and took Max's hand. He didn't dare look at her, but his whole arm tingled from the contact.

When the group had finished the grand tour of the first floor and taken their seats at the imposing dining table, Vespa beamed at them all.

"So, what do you think?" she asked.

"Nice crib," said Tremaine. He leaned back, interlacing his fingers behind his head. "Does it have cable TV?"

"Why are we here?" asked Max again.

Vespa aimed her wide brown eyes at him. "You mean, you don't know?"

"Um, no?" said Wyatt, blushing furiously. He was easily as tongue-tied as Max around Vespa da Costa.

Their hostess swiveled to Hantai Annie. "Well, as I told Mrs. Wong—"

"Annie," said the spymaster.

"The government was going to confiscate this house and all LOTUS assets—which would've thrown me into foster care."

Several of the orphans winced sympathetically.

Vespa shrugged. "But as it turns out, Mrs. Helen Frost's only surviving relative is . . . me. Hantai Annie talked to her government contacts, and, well, I'm inheriting the house and cars."

Max gave an appreciative whistle.

"Big whoop," said Nikki, eyeing the platters of food being carried in by servers. "Bully for you, Little Miss Rich Girl."

"No," said Vespa with a mischievous wink. "Bully for *you*."

Wyatt's brow crinkled. "I don't get it."

"Because I'm underage, I need a guardian," said Vespa. "And what better guardian than the director of an orphanage?"

Cinnabar squinted at her suspiciously. "You mean . . ."

Hantai Annie spread her arms wide. *"Minna*, welcome to you new home!"

Gasps of disbelief greeted her revelation. Max gaped. Here? They were going to live *here*?

"Today, we sign one-hundred-year lease," said the spymaster. "This is now officially School For S.P.I.E.S."

Cheers exploded from the group. Tremaine and Rashid hooted, banging their cups on the table. Max's chest swelled with warmth, like a balloon filling with breath. They would have a home, a stable home at last, for as long as they wanted it. He glanced across the table at his father, and a thought struck him.

"But what about my dad?" he asked, looking between Hantai Annie and Simon. "Will he be here too?"

Her ebony eyes twinkled. "Just so happens, this school is one teacher short. And if Mr. Segredo is willing . . . ?"

Simon Segredo's gaze traveled the table, taking in the ragtag bunch. "To teach these ruffians?" he said. "To put up with their disobedience, incessant quarreling, and insufferable cheekiness?" He frowned, and Max felt his stomach clench.

The frown transformed into a beaming smile. "It would be my honor."

Max met and held his father's gaze. So this is what family feels like, he thought. How about that?

After lunch, when the crew had split up to explore the house and all its secrets, Max drew his father aside into one of the many sitting rooms. Everything seemed to be going so well, but something was troubling him.

"I've been thinking," he said.

"Yes?" asked Simon.

Max waved a hand at the paneled walls, immaculate fireplace, and posh fixtures. "The whole time I was living here undercover, all I wanted was to be a normal kid, with a normal family. And now . . ."

His father nodded encouragingly.

"Now that we're all back together, I can't help thinking that what caused all this trouble in the first place was the whole spy thing," said Max. He couldn't look at his father. "It . . . it drove you away, it killed Mum, and—" He cleared his throat. "And it nearly got me stuck living with a monster."

Ever so gently, Simon reached out and touched Max's arm. "I would never have let that happen."

"But my point is, well . . . maybe I shouldn't be a spy."

His dad's eyebrows climbed his forehead. "What?"

Twisting one hand in the other, Max forged on. "What if . . . I dunno, maybe I should try being a normal kid instead. No spying, no secret missions, just school and family. You know, regular stuff."

He glanced up into his father's eyes and the tenderness he saw there made his throat close up.

"Max," said Simon. "You are a truly special kid, you know that? And now that we're together again, I won't let anything tear us apart."

Max nodded. He didn't trust his voice.

"If you want to give up spying, that's your right, and I fully support you in that." His dad took a breath. "But . . ."

"But?" said Max.

Simon laid his hand on his son's shoulder. "Normal is highly overrated."

"Huh?"

"You're not normal," he said.

Max winced. "Thanks a lot."

"By that I mean you are incredibly gifted at this thing we do—much more so than I ever was. After all, you have a double dose of spy DNA. You can give it up, yes. But if you quit now, you'll miss out on all the good stuff."

Curiosity sparked in Max, despite his intentions. "Good stuff?"

Slow as melting butter, a smile spread across his father's

face. "Yes, indeed. You've learned a bit, but you've only scratched the surface."

"Well," said Max. "Maybe I could put off my decision for a *little* longer."

"That's my boy."

A thought occurred to him. "And while I'm still being a spy, maybe you can help me with something?"

"Name it."

Max raked a hand through his hair. "The mind-control device. Even though I agreed to, it's been bugging me that I just handed it over to Mr. Elbow. It's a dangerous tool."

"It is," said his father, the light of understanding dawning in his eyes.

"And I was thinking, maybe we could . . ."

"Steal it back and destroy it?"

"Well," said Max, "yeah."

Simon's eyes gleamed. "Sounds like a perfect father-son project."

They turned as one and set off to rejoin the others. "First thing we need," said Max's father, "is a good team. . . ."

"Funny," said Max, "but I think I might know where to find one."

SPY TRAINING—Making a Dead Drop Without Getting Caught

Popular for nearly as long as spies have been around, a dead drop is a way of secretly passing items between two people. You know those scenes in the movies where two people sit down at a table with briefcases and surreptitiously switch them? That's not it. Since both people are present, it's considered a *live drop*.

A dead drop, however, means that both agents don't need to be there to make the exchange. In fact, the two parties don't even have to know each other—all they need to know is the drop location and signaling device. This offers a way of avoiding personal meetings, which can jeopardize the spy network if the agents are observed or caught.

Give me a sign
Whoever plans to pick up your item needs to know when it's in place. That's where signals come in handy. A signal could be anything agreed upon by the two agents in advance—a chalk mark on a wall, a Post-it in a window, a shade pulled down, or a statue wearing a goofy hat.

Bear in mind that everyone and his brother can see your signal, so writing the words "dead drop" with an arrow pointing under the park bench where you've hidden your package might be just a tad obvious. Subtlety is key here. In fact, the signal doesn't even need to appear near the drop—merely in a place where your co-conspirator will see it.

For example, if you wanted to leave a key to let a friendly agent into your home, you might make a chalk mark on the door, letting them know that the key is under the flowerpot around the side of the house.

Do the dead drop

To make a successful dead drop, here are three things for the trainee spy to bear in mind:

1. Pick the right spot.
You want to make sure not to draw unwanted attention, either to the drop-off and pickup, or to the package itself when unattended. Popular locations include a hole in a tree, behind a loose brick, inside a cutout library book (an unpopular book, of course!), or beneath a park bench. By contrast, leaving the package outside a police station or airport will only land you in deep, deep doo-doo. Choose wisely.

2. Make sure it blends in.
Whatever you're leaving in the dead drop should either be out of sight enough to go unnoticed or so much a part of the scene that it gets overlooked. A suspicious-looking package taped to a wall stands out. But a fake rock in a yard blends in with all the real rocks around it.

Along those lines, make sure your hiding spot isn't too obvious. Leaving a key under the welcome mat? A rookie mistake. Leaving a key in an empty soda can under the hedge? Much more spy-worthy.

3. Use protection.
If you're hiding something in the ground or behind a trash bin, you want to make sure it's still in usable shape by the time your contact picks it up. Ever since the sixties, real spies have been using dead-drop spikes, a waterproof concealment device that

hides money, microfilm, documents, and other items. But if you can't make it to the spy store and have to improvise, any water-proof container will do.

Best of luck, and remember the spy's Number One rule of dead drops: don't get caught with your hand in the cookie jar.

Excerpted from:
Survival Skills for the Modern Spy, 3rd Edition
by Giacomo Fleming, Belle Maclean, and S. Gromonowitz

**For more spy information and activities,
please visit www.school4spies.com.**

ACKNOWLEDGMENTS

TO SUCCEED on his mission, every spy needs a top-flight support team. A writer is no different. This time around, I'm particularly grateful for the eagle eye and terrific story sense of my editor, Stephanie Lurie, who helped me through a rough patch of the writing and asked the questions I hadn't even thought to ask.

Thanks also to my technical consultants, Peter Selvaggio (security matters) and Mick Guinn (computer hacking), for helping this nontechie understand what's what. Major mahalos go out to Terry Sheldon (beta reader and British slang), Annie Sung Bernstein and Janette Cross (Japanese), and Carol Bond (Aussie slang). Your comments were invaluable.

And finally, a Blofeld volcano–size thank-you to my wife, Janette, for all her patience, support, and understanding. Living with a writer is no easy task, and you manage it with grace to spare.

Don't miss the first two books in the School for S.P.I.E.S. series!

PLAYING WITH FIRE

Max Segredo learns the meaning of family when he is sent to the Merry Sunshine Orphanage, a front for a spy organization.

"Between training exercises, Max's search for his father, secret missions, and double agents, the action never stops. This book will appeal to both boys and girls. Characters are diverse and well thought out. The School for S.P.I.E.S. series will be a winner. Highly recommended."
—*Library Media Connection*

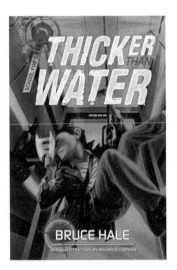

THICKER THAN WATER

How can Max keep his family together when the School for S.P.I.E.S. is threatened by forces both within and without?

Coming next from Bruce Hale:

MONSTERTOWN MYSTERY
BOOK ONE:

CURSE OF THE WERE-HYENA

*Only Carlos and his best friend Benny know
the truth: their favorite teacher has been bitten
by a were-hyena! Unless they can find a cure
before the next full moon, they'll have a lot
more than pop quizzes to worry about. . . .*